"I think I shou

Gabe slipped ins[...] lock. "Parnell's p[...]

Dallas put her ha[...]

"If you have an ext[...] and blanket, I'll park on your sofa."

Staying in her trailer all night? Dallas tried to imagine how that would work, with her hormones raging every time she looked at this tall cowboy. She gazed up at him, her heart hammering in her chest. Why not just take him into her bed and be done with it?

Because they were all wrong for each other.

She retrieved a pillow and blanket from the closet and thrust them at him. "Here."

He turned and tossed the pillow onto the sofa. "Good night, Dallas."

She left the room and walked down the hall, trying in vain to suppress the need coursing through her. She closed her bedroom door with more force than necessary.

"Don't lock it," he called out. "You might need me during the night."

She knew he'd said that on purpose.

Vicki Lewis Thompson couldn't resist writing a story with a country-and-western theme. She and her husband recently joined the line dance craze and have become experts at the Electric Slide and the Boot Scootin' Boogie! To get her in the mood for creating a cowboy story, Vicki listened to a CD of Western movie themes as she wrote. So, pull out your ol' country tunes and enjoy reading *The Bounty Hunter!*

Don't miss Vicki's upcoming miniseries about three city slickers who try their hand at being cowboys, available in 1995.

Books by Vicki Lewis Thompson

HARLEQUIN TEMPTATION
374—IT HAPPENED ONE WEEKEND
396—ANYTHING GOES
410—ASK DR. KATE
439—FOOLS RUSH IN
484—LOVERBOY
502—WEDDING SONG

THE BOUNTY HUNTER

VICKI LEWIS THOMPSON

Harlequin Books

TORONTO • NEW YORK • LONDON
AMSTERDAM • PARIS • SYDNEY • HAMBURG
STOCKHOLM • ATHENS • TOKYO • MILAN
MADRID • WARSAW • BUDAPEST • AUCKLAND

To Birgit Davis-Todd,
for her editorial savvy, aid and comfort
through the years.

ISBN 0-373-25616-7

THE BOUNTY HUNTER

Copyright © 1994 by Vicki Lewis Thompson.

Printed in U.S.A.

1

ANYTIME TWO-DOZEN red roses arrived, Dallas Wade liked to know why.

She had no reason to expect the extravagant bouquet awaiting her Friday night when she arrived at Rowdy Ranch, Tucson's premiere country-western night spot. She ran one of five mall-type shops located in a corner of the complex, whose main attraction was a large dance floor. The scent of roses engulfed her as she entered the shop, an exclusive hairstyling salon for men.

Her assistant, Amber Dalton, dressed to match Dallas in fringed shorts, boots, snug western shirt and hat, tucked a stack of towels into a dark-paneled cabinet. "You must have given some guy one heck of a haircut."

Dallas pulled the small envelope from its plastic holder. "I can't imagine what these are for."

"And here you were telling me there's nobody special right now."

"There isn't. I really don't..." Dallas stared at the enclosed card. *Thanks for believing in me. Neal Parnell.*

"So?" Amber leaned over her shoulder. "Who's the secret admirer?" She paused and read the card. "My God, Dallas. Neal Parnell. Did you speak to him personally or something after the trial?"

"No, of course not." Dallas tried to fit the strange gesture into a logical framework. "But considering I was foreperson of the jury, he might think I was somehow responsible for finding him not guilty."

"Maybe. But how would he know where you worked?"

Dallas thought back over the trial. "He was sitting right there when the jury was chosen, and we had to give our names and occupations." She met Amber's concerned gaze. "I suppose he could have called around this afternoon, looking for me."

Amber shivered. "That gives me the creeps. After all, he was on trial for rape."

"And he was acquitted." Dallas looked Amber straight in the eye. "He had a fair trial. He was found innocent. Now he should be treated like everyone else."

"Yeah, but if he called salons until he found out where you worked—that's sort of weird, don't you think?"

"Not if he had some secretary at the dealership do it for him."

Amber glanced at the flowers and slowly nodded. "You're right. And after all the money his father spent on that shark of a lawyer, what's a few more bucks for roses? Parnell Motors probably treated this like the conclusion of a big business deal or something, with gifts of gratitude passed out all around."

"That's discrimination." Dallas was irritated by Amber's "shark lawyer" assessment. Her assistant was subtly implying Dallas and the jury had been duped, when, in fact, the prosecution had had no case. She turned to hang up her fringed jacket. "The press coverage was discriminatory, too. You're prejudiced because he's rich."

"You're darned right I am. From all reports, he's a party animal who's probably never worked a full day in all his twenty-six years. That's enough information for me to write him off."

Dallas held on to her temper and turned slowly back to Amber. "But it doesn't make him a criminal."

Amber shook her head and grinned. "That's just like you, Dallas. You're so damned unbiased that you should make a career of jury service."

"No, thanks." Dallas knew Amber didn't really intend to needle her. She just enjoyed speaking her mind, a quality Dallas appreciated most of the time. "I missed going through my usual routine these past few days," she added, meaning it. She wanted to put the trial behind her.

Amber stroked one silky rose petal and leaned forward to sniff the heady fragrance. "Gonna keep these?"

"No, I'm not." Dallas ripped the card and envelope into four neat parts and tossed them into the trash. "Sending me flowers for doing my civic duty is inappropriate. He's probably so excited about being acquitted he's not thinking, but it just looks bad. Like a payoff or something."

"Then let me have them. I can drive Vince crazy wondering who sent them to me."

"Fine, as long as you take them out to your car right now." Dallas picked up the heavy vase and started to hand it to her.

"Don't tell me they're not your color," said a male voice from the doorway of the shop.

Dallas glanced around and looked straight into the blue eyes of Neal Parnell.

GABE ESCALANTE PUSHED open the heavy oak doors of Rowdy Ranch and was greeted by a Dolly Parton song on the sound system. The bouncer waved him through. Nobody had ever checked Gabe's ID, not even when he was underage.

Once inside he shoved back his hat and surveyed the complex. He immediately spotted Parnell talking to a tall blonde in fringed black shorts, red boots and blouse and a red Stetson. Gabe's eyes narrowed. The sexy outfit changed her some, but he could swear she was the one his sister had pointed out as the foreman—no, they called them fore*persons* now—of the jury. And she held a vase stuffed with roses.

Parnell was all duded up in western gear—a loud cowboy shirt, tight black jeans, a black hat. Gabe wondered if this was a hangout for the guy. How convenient that the fore*person* of the jury just happened to be a woman, and happened to work here.

Gabe ambled toward them in the nonchalant way he'd perfected over the years. He wanted to find out where the flowers had come from, but there was no need to get anybody excited. Yet.

He hadn't been inside Rowdy Ranch in years. Back when he was a kid the building had been a discount warehouse. The place was huge, with enough room for a large racetrack-style dance floor, three bars, at least fifteen pool tables and a slew of pinball machines and video games. The new management had replaced the live band with a deejay booth that loosely resembled a stagecoach and had set up an inexpensive all-you-can-eat buffet. Gelled lights and two revolving mirrored balls flung rainbows over the dance floor, and neon glowed from every wall.

The place wasn't crowded yet, but in a few hours Gabe knew it would be packed. "Rowdy Ranch—where spurs jingle and folks mingle," warbled the radio ads. The country-western dance craze had transformed Rowdy Ranch from a struggling cowboy hangout into the most popular nightclub in town.

The mall-style concessions in the far corner were something new, too. The leather shop selling boots and hats made sense to him, and the old-fashioned photography studio where people dressed up like gamblers and dance-hall women seemed logical. Western shirts, jewelry and tourist-trap pottery always made money. But the Cutting Pen, where Parnell was, puzzled Gabe. Even though the atmosphere was masculine, with lariats, spurs and ten-gallon hats hanging on the walls, what kind of guy would get his hair shampooed and cut in front of a dance hall full of people?

Three pool tables, all unoccupied, squatted in front of the row of shops. Gabe headed for the one closest to the Cutting Pen and pulled a cue stick from the rack. He took his time examining the tip and sighting down the stick while he listened to Parnell and the woman.

"I watched you during the trial," Parnell said. "I could tell you weren't buying that crap the prosecuting attorney was dishing out."

"I just tried to be fair," the woman replied. Her voice was low and well modulated, a kind of voice that pleasantly stroked Gabe's nerve endings. In another context he might spend the evening trying to find out if the woman matched the quality of her voice—but not tonight.

"Oh, you were the fairest of them all, Dallas," Parnell said. "That's why I sent the flowers."

Gabe's jaws clamped together. So the son of a bitch had sent them. Flowers to the foreperson of the jury, a woman he seemed to be on a first-name basis with. The cue stick trembled in Gabe's hands. He laid it on the green felt and gripped the edge of the table to steady himself. Everything depended on his keeping his cool. He walked toward the bar, away from the cozy pair. He'd heard enough.

He'd wait until Parnell left. Then he'd get a haircut in that ridiculous place, so he could find out something about this woman named Dallas. Maybe Parnell had bought her off. Maybe he'd bribed the entire jury. If so, Gabe would find out. He would poke and probe into every action Parnell had taken and would take in the future. And somehow, someday, Gabe would nail the bastard. The jury may have decided differently today, but as sure as rattlesnakes had fangs, Neal Parnell had raped his sister.

"THE FLOWERS WEREN'T necessary, Mr. Parnell," Dallas said, fighting a nervous flutter in her stomach. "I was only doing the job I was assigned to do."

"Call me Neal. And I don't believe a word of it. A lot of people on that jury wanted my head on a pole. It would have made a great scandal and people love scandal. But you were different. I'll bet you talked some people into changing their minds."

She had, but she decided not to say so. "They could see the evidence was lacking."

"Because you pointed it out. I'd say I owe you dinner at the Tack Room. When are you free?"

Over Parnell's shoulder Dallas could see Amber's wide eyes and gaping mouth. The Tack Room was Tucson's only five-star restaurant, and she and Amber joked about going there when they won the lottery.

"You don't owe me a thing, Neal," Dallas said gently.

"Then let's do it for the hell of it."

"I think it would be better if we didn't."

He looked confused. Then his expression cleared. "Oh, I get it. You think people will talk. You're not used to that. Listen, Dallas, you have to say to hell with public opinion and enjoy yourself." He pointed a finger at her. "I can see you work way too hard. Take a break. Have some fun for a change."

Dallas could understand why Neal was unpopular with the public. He flaunted his indolence as if it were a virtue. Parnell Motors, a family business for three generations, provided him with a pseudosales job, but nobody believed Neal put in long hours on the car lot. Yet he drove a black Corvette, ate at the finest restaurants, dressed in the best clothes. Working people had a hard time with that sort of unearned life-style.

Dallas gave him her firm-but-friendly brush-off. "I don't think so, Neal." She smiled, but her tone didn't leave room for discussion.

He laughed. "Okay, I can see you're spooked by this trial business, but people will forget about that, and you'll be able to relax. In the meantime I'll hang around." He touched the brim of his hat. "You're worth waiting for, ma'am." He turned and headed for the dance floor, where a few people had begun a spirited line dance.

Dallas watched as he inserted himself into the group. He didn't know the dance, but he quickly coaxed a woman in a short denim skirt into teaching him.

Amber came to stand beside her. "Looks like Rowdy Ranch just landed another regular customer."

Dallas sighed as she thought of trying to fend Neal off night after night.

"And I'll bet he's not used to being turned down for dinner at the Tack Room."

"Probably not." Dallas glanced toward her. "Listen, one of us needs to hit the buffet line and get something to eat. I'll cover the shop if you want to go first."

"Sure. Signal if you need me."

Dallas watched Amber walk toward the long buffet table. Several of the cowboys gathering at the bar watched her, too. Amber was good for business. They both worked Friday and Saturday nights to allow each other breaks during the nonstop activity that would begin in about another half hour. Dallas had hired Amber seven months ago when it became obvious the customer load demanded it. She and Amber traded off weeknights.

She'd chosen Amber primarily for her excellent hairstyling skills, but also for her great legs. Men paid a fair amount of change for a shampoo and haircut at the Cutting Pen and Dallas had found they paid it willingly if the stylist wore shorts to good advantage. She was idealistic enough to wish the world were different, and practical enough to accept that it wasn't.

"Open for business?"

Dallas snapped out of her reverie. The man leaning against the far side of the wide entrance had approached silently. She glanced at his scuffed ostrich-skin boots, worn jeans and faded blue plaid shirt, sleeves rolled to the elbow, and decided that he dressed this way all the time, not just to fit into the atmosphere at Rowdy Ranch.

His skin was darkened by the sun, and beneath the brim of his black hat the strength of his features reminded her of an Aztec warrior she'd seen depicted once on a mural in Mexico City. His dark hair curled down past his nape. This man hadn't seen the inside of a barber shop, let alone a styling salon, for at least three months.

"Have a seat," she said, giving him a careful smile that welcomed, yet drew boundaries around that welcome. She allowed herself to be a man's fantasy for the time he rested within her chair. Her customers seemed to understand the unspoken rules and she'd rarely had a problem with unwanted advances. Amber hadn't yet perfected the technique, but Dallas was slowly teaching her.

The man hung his hat on a rack by the door and sat in the chair gingerly. He was probably the sort of guy who paid a bare minimum to a male barber whenever some woman heckled him into getting a haircut. Dallas wondered why he was here. Maybe to settle a bet or prove he could handle anything. Dallas suspected he'd worked himself up to the experience, possibly even had a couple of drinks to bolster his courage.

She turned the chair to face the mirror. "I'll need your name."

He frowned. "Why?"

"For my files, so I can record what we did tonight. Then next time I'll remember your preferences." The subtle suggestion there would be a next time was one of her time-honored techniques for getting repeat business.

"Gabe." He cleared his throat and looked slightly uncomfortable. "Gabe Escalante."

"What a wonderful name."

He made no response as she copied it onto an index card, but when she glanced into the mirror he'd composed his expression so that he once more resembled a haughty warrior prince from another age. She wondered again what had motivated him to come into her salon.

She accepted his reticence as a challenge. "Just relax," she said, picking up the massage wand and running it across his shoulder blades. His facial expression didn't change, but his muscles flexed uneasily beneath the soft shirt. Lots of muscles. "I'll bet you work outdoors," she said.

"Some."

Dallas smiled. The strong, silent type still existed, but she could usually break them down a little during the time she had them in her chair. "Construction?" The vibrating wand was having an effect and the tense set of his shoulders eased a fraction. She imagined a softening of the flintlike dark eyes.

"Not exactly."

"The mines, then." She moved the wand in a semi-circle beneath his shoulder blades, working through the knots.

"Once upon a time."

Dallas thought she heard him sigh, which told her she was making progress. Men who had a sensual experience in her salon always came back. She'd consider it a feather in her cap if she captured this stressed-out cowboy. "I have a brother who worked out at Duval. When the bottom dropped out of the copper market he was laid off, like a lot of miners." Dallas flipped off the switch on the wand and laid it on the counter beside her. "Times are tough."

"Not for everyone." He sounded bitter, almost as though he were insinuating something.

Dallas wondered what he could be getting at, but shrugged it off. She pulled a cape patterned to look like rawhide around him and lifted up his hair to snap it at his nape. He immediately freed his arms from under the cape and gripped the arms of the chair. He was back on guard, but she'd soon fix that.

She ran her fingers up through the back of his hair, lightly caressing his scalp. The texture was surprisingly silky. He had good volume. He'd take a styling cut well, if he'd let her experiment a little. "How much are we taking off tonight?"

That comment usually brought some harmless joking from her customers, but Gabe seemed at a loss for words. Some powerful energy radiated from him, though, coaxing her to stroke through his hair again, although she had no professional reason to. "I'd recommend some layering, to show off that natural curl."

The choked sound he made could have been laughter or distress.

Dallas chose to interpret it as laughter. She met his gaze in the mirror and smiled. "Okay, Gabe. I know you're not used to this sort of place, but bear with me. You'll be glad you did."

The look he gave her was direct and strong, shocking her as if she'd stepped from an air-conditioned building into the hot Arizona sunshine. She didn't often meet a man with such a self-confident gaze. It was a quality she'd nurtured in herself, and for a moment she and Gabe seemed to understand each other perfectly, although no words were spoken. A man who could match her strength. She'd about given up finding one.

GABE STARED at the blond Amazon in the mirror and wondered what the hell he'd gotten himself into. This woman wasn't at all what he'd expected. She seemed so self-possessed and sure of herself he couldn't picture her stooping to consort with the likes of Parnell. But she'd said times were tough, and she was trying to keep a business going. Maybe Parnell had offered her financial help.

It became more difficult to think straight with every moment in this chair. He'd been on a plane for thirty-six hours in an attempt to get back to Tucson for at least some of the trial, only to arrive at the courthouse after it was all over. That would work to his advantage because neither Parnell nor this woman could tie him to

Celia. But he hadn't taken a break since leaving Celia at the courthouse. He was jet-lagged and emotionally whipped. He looked away from the mirror before Dallas could see any vulnerability in his gaze.

"I'm going to tilt you back, so I can shampoo and condition your hair," she said in that sultry voice of hers.

"You don't have to do that."

"It's part of what you pay for, Gabe." She moved a lever and he didn't have much choice except to lean back. She slipped a soft towel under his neck to cushion the porcelain basin. "I'll bet you're a man who likes to get his money's worth."

Well, she had that right. And his tax money hadn't bought him much when it came to putting away a slimeball like Parnell. He'd better concentrate on why he was lounging in this fancy excuse for a barber shop. Except concentrating wasn't easy when she ran warm water over his scalp and massaged something creamy into his hair. Nobody had washed his hair since . . . he couldn't remember. When he was a little kid on the ranch, maybe, except that had probably been in a horse trough, and designed for efficiency, not pleasure.

And pleasure described what Dallas was giving him. His eyes refused to stay open as her clever fingers worked the lather through in long, kneading motions that nearly made him groan with delight. She leaned over him, her breasts tantalizingly close, her lush perfume filling his nostrils. And he'd wondered why men subjected themselves to this.

The running water subdued the sounds of country music, the voices from the bar and the crack of a cue ball on the tables nearby until they were nothing but inconsequential background noise. Gabe was totally immersed in the experience of having this woman minister to him. She'd stopped talking, and for the life of him he couldn't summon the energy to speak.

Warm water sluiced through his hair, followed by a caressing motion of her hand. To his disappointment she turned off the water, but she rubbed his wet hair with long, languorous strokes of the towel, and the mood remained.

"That's better," she murmured. "I'll lever you back up now."

As she raised the chair he opened his eyes and the first thing he saw was the damned flowers. The sensuous haze evaporated as he stared at them. She must have noticed his gaze because she swiveled him toward the mirror with more vigor than he thought necessary. She didn't want him focusing on those flowers. Guilty conscience, perhaps?

He glanced in the mirror, but she was busy choosing a comb from the sterilizing jar on the counter. Or maybe she didn't want to look at him right now. The party, sweet though it might have been, was over. Time for him to do a little questioning of his own.

"Will you let me use my own judgment on the style?" she asked as she combed his damp hair back from his forehead.

"Sure."

"Good. I think you'll like the results."

He decided to go for the jugular. "Is Neal Parnell one of your regular customers?"

She froze in mid-motion. Then she began studiously snipping at his hair. "No. Why do you ask?"

"I saw him in here a while ago."

"Yes." Her voice had lost its soothing texture. Such a pity.

"I wouldn't think having him hang around would be very good for business."

"He can go wherever he wants." Her snipping became more vigorous. "He's an innocent man."

"So the jury said."

She stopped snipping and glared at him in the mirror. "Were you at the trial?"

"Got there after it was over, unfortunately. But someone pointed you out as the foreperson."

Her chin went up a notch. "That's right."

He jerked a thumb back toward the vase of roses. "Nice flowers."

She laid down the scissors and the comb. "Just what are you implying, Mr. Escalante?"

He'd meant to be more subtle, but exhaustion pushed him toward the accusation he'd been restraining for hours. "No implication. The plain truth. You turned a rapist loose."

"That's not true!"

"Oh, yes, it is." He wrenched off the cape, scattering hair, and pushed himself out of the chair. "And for a little reward, he sends you flowers. What else has Neal Parnell done for you lately, Miss Dallas?"

Her face went dead white and she began to tremble. "Get out of my shop."

"Sure thing." He pulled money from his wallet and threw it on the counter. Then he snatched his hat from the rack. "But justice is a hobby of mine. And I'm not going away."

2

DALLAS DIDN'T MOVE as Gabe stormed out of the shop. Then she grabbed a broom and began furiously sweeping the bits of dark hair that had scattered when Gabe pulled off the cape.

"Dallas?"

She looked up to find Dave Fogarty, operator of the old-time photography concession, standing in the doorway.

"Did that fellow cause a problem?"

Dallas gripped the broom handle and took a deep breath. "No."

Dave stroked his full gray beard. "I've never seen anybody take off like that from your shop. Usually they leave looking sort of dazed."

"I ordered him out."

Amber hurried in, carrying a half-full mug of coffee that she nearly spilled in her haste. "You did *what*? Did he try to hit on you or something?"

"No." More in control now, Dallas took the dustpan from a corner and swept the snippets of dark hair into it.

"Hey, Dallas," Dave said. "I've been running the shop across from yours for eighteen months, and I've never known you to throw somebody out. What did he do?"

Dallas dumped the contents of the dustpan in the trash and faced them. "He accused me of having some underhanded deal with Parnell, of somehow rigging the trial."

Amber gasped. "Oh, wow. He's lucky he didn't go out of here looking like van Gogh."

"I considered aiming the scissors a bit lower than that."

Dave adjusted his gray Stetson down over his eyes. "He's at the bar. Maybe I'll go have a little talk with him."

"No, please." Dallas picked up the cape from the floor and folded it. "Let's not make this into a bigger deal than it is."

"That darn Parnell would have to come in here." Amber glanced nervously at the vase of roses. "I suppose the guy figured out about the flowers, too."

Dave's eyebrows rose. "Parnell sent you those?"

"Unfortunately. He has some idea that as foreperson of the jury I deserve his gratitude."

"That's not all he thinks you deserve," Amber said. "He's developed a crush on you, Dallas. I watched him while I was eating dinner, and in between dances he kept looking over at the shop." She turned to Dave. "He invited her to dinner at the Tack Room."

Dave let out a low whistle.

"She declined."

"That's good." Dave glanced back at his studio where a couple lingered, looking at the sepia-toned photographs on display. "I'd better get back, but I'll keep an eye on you over here. If either of those clowns pester you again, I'll drop by."

"Thanks, Dave."

Amber put down her coffee and started toward the roses. "Maybe I'd better take those out to my car before they cause any more trouble."

"Wait. I know I promised them to you, but I'd appreciate it if you'd leave them here, after all."

"You *want* these flowers?"

"No, but I refuse to be intimidated by that son of a bitch." Dallas glared out the door of the shop. "Those roses are staying until they wilt. Just let him try and make something out of it!"

GABE KNEW he'd screwed up. He sat at the bar where he had a view of the Cutting Pen and nursed a beer. Alcohol probably wasn't such a great idea, either, but the crisp bite of the ice-cold liquid fit the bill right now.

He'd done everything wrong. His plan had been to get a haircut and some information. To cooly, calmly lead Dallas into some sort of compromising confession. What had gone wrong?

Just about everything.

He should have refused the massage. Refused the shampoo. Refused to meet the laughing challenge in her eyes, gray eyes with little flecks of gold that sparkled when she smiled. He'd become fascinated with the spirit reflected in those eyes, had wanted to study them far too long. In spite of damning evidence that she was dishonest, he'd begun to *like* her. Not to mention the baser emotions her touch stirred in him.

Apparently imagining this desirable woman dealing with Parnell had been too much for him. Instead of questioning, he'd accused. Instead of playing it cool, he'd worked himself into a hot rage. He could blame it on lack of sleep, on the frustration of not being there for Celia during the trial, on the fury blasting through him when he'd heard the verdict.

He could sit here and make excuses all night, but he'd ruined Dallas as a source of information. And if she was cozy with Parnell, she'd tip him off before the evening was over. Parnell might even have the resources to uncover Gabe's identity as Celia's brother, even though they no longer had the same last name.

His lack of judgment could mean that Parnell would slip through his fingers. If that happened, he'd never forgive himself.

"Another beer?" the bartender asked.

Gabe nodded. The bartender had been eyeing him strangely ever since he sat down. He scratched inside his collar where sharp barbs of hair had fallen when he'd pulled the cape away. He knew his hat didn't disguise the fact that he had half of a haircut, and he probably looked pretty stupid. But stupid-looking or not, he'd keep an eye on Parnell for the rest of the night. And Dallas.

She moved with the short, jerky gestures of anger that he recognized in himself. She was probably relaying the whole story to the photography-shop guy and the other woman, a brunette with long, straight hair and a figure almost as good as Dallas's. Gabe shook his head, angry at himself all over again. He should have known that after months of being without sex he'd be susceptible to a beautiful woman's attention.

And Dallas was breathtaking, with hair the color of aspen leaves in the fall. When she moved, the curls cascading down her back shimmered the way aspen leaves danced in a breeze. But he'd lived in the world long enough to know that beautiful hair and a great body could just as easily be decorating treachery as honesty.

Another man walked into the shop, took off his cowboy hat and eased into the chair Gabe had vacated. Dallas reached for the massage wand, and Gabe flexed his shoulders, remembering how soothing the deep vibration had felt. When Dallas tipped the man back into the shampoo bowl, Gabe could feel her fingers on his scalp, smell the fragrance of her skin. He was definitely turned on, not a good condition to be in right now.

He looked away, distracting himself by examining the updated decor of Rowdy Ranch. On the wall behind the deejay booth a black metal sculpture of wild horses was backlit in red. On another, a stagecoach backlit in blue careened across the desert, the driver's whip a vivid slash of purple neon. The untamed West. Leave your inhibitions behind.

But he was here to monitor Parnell, and he'd better remember that. Spotting him in the crowd wasn't hard. His gaudy dress and loud manner made him easy to find. He'd already bought some new friends by making a big deal out of paying for a round of drinks.

Gabe was taking the first shift of watching Parnell, but he'd lined up two guys to spell him. They were working cheap because they were friends of his and they didn't like Parnell's kind, but Gabe would have paid his last penny to snare this particular lowlife. Celia deserved to see him behind bars, along with anyone who had helped him get away with his crimes. If that included the beautiful Dallas, so be it.

IT WAS THE LONGEST Friday night in history for Dallas. She closed the shop at midnight. Amber had gone home a half hour earlier, and Dave had a run of business and would obviously be staying late. Dallas didn't feel like waiting around so he could walk her to the parking lot, as he often did and undoubtedly wanted to do tonight. But she was a big girl, and she always carried a small canister of pepper spray in her purse for the times she left the dance hall alone.

Following her usual precaution, she pulled the spray out once she pushed through the oak doors into the night. She wore her fringed leather jacket, but the late February chill nipped at her bare legs. When she saw the black Corvette parked several spaces down from her truck, she wondered if it could be Neal's.

She was too mentally and physically exhausted to care, but as far as she knew, he was still dancing. The Aztec warrior had been glued to his bar stool. She'd passed him with her head high, her eyes forward, and silently wished him a vicious hangover in the morning.

To think that she'd thought herself mildly attracted to that arrogant man. She wondered if he was some sort of vigilante type who ran around second-guessing judges and juries. For all she knew he was dangerous. She got a firmer grip on her spray as she unlocked the door of her pickup.

Just as she was about to get in, a car swerved up next to her. She whirled, her thumb on the trigger of the spray.

"Hey, don't shoot!" said the driver of the black Corvette.

Dallas looked closer and recognized Neal. It had been his car, after all, and now he was heading home. "A woman can't be too careful in a parking lot late at night," Dallas said, lowering the spray slightly.

"Yeah, I suppose you'll be especially careful after listening to the testimony of that woman at the trial."

"That's right." Dallas turned to get into the truck. "Good night now."

"You know we could just have a drink sometime. I looked for you during your breaks, but I couldn't find you."

Dallas had spent her breaks in the women's rest room for that very reason. Dodging Neal all night was one of the reasons she was so tired. "I don't think we'll be having a drink, Neal," she said, and swung into the truck.

"Don't be too sure," he called out, just before he peeled out in a cloud of dust that settled over the peacock blue finish of Dallas's truck.

Cursing under her breath, Dallas started the engine. Then she noticed another truck pull out and drive in the same direction as Neal's Corvette. She had a strong suspicion the battered old pickup belonged to the Aztec warrior. Well, at least he was following Neal instead of her.

The trip to her mobile home in Avra Valley seemed to take much longer than the twenty minutes her dashboard clock registered. Once there she pulled into the dirt driveway and parked under the dusk-to-dawn light she'd installed last week, before the trial had begun eating up all her spare time.

Behind a high chain-link fence, Gretchen, her Great Dane, barked a greeting. Dallas checked automatically to make sure both her horses, a bay mare named Sugar and a roan gelding named Spice, stood peacefully in the pipe corral. A three-quarter moon puddled cacti shadows on the desert floor and outlined the clefts of canyons in the nearby Tucson Mountains. Tomorrow she'd go for a ride into one of those canyons, the first outing she'd had time for since the trial.

Gretchen started whining, and a large form detached itself from the edge of the fence. Dallas leaped from the truck, the pepper spray in her hand. "Get out of here, Igor!" she shouted.

A huge dog, half Irish wolfhound, half Saint Bernard, bounded away down the road. Dallas was glad he'd left of his own accord. She didn't want to use the spray on him, but he was making a real nuisance of himself.

Adrenaline still pumping, Dallas locked the truck and strode toward the gate. Gretchen whined and yipped, trying to get out. "And you, you harlot, get away from that gate. He's not for you."

Gretchen barked once in protest, but she backed away from the gate as Dallas unlocked it.

"I know in your present condition you don't understand this," Dallas said, rubbing the dog's large head. "But you're meant for better things than that mongrel.

I'm saving you for Mr. Right, who will be so purebred he'll probably bring a valet when he comes calling."

Gretchen licked her hand and trotted beside her up the flagstone path, which Dallas had laid last summer before the rains. Her list of projects was long, but each one completed gave her immense satisfaction because she was building her life herself, without depending on anyone else, least of all some man.

She unlocked the dead bolt on her front door and stepped into the living room she'd furnished bit by bit as she could afford it. The sofa and easy chair were upholstered in blue denim, and she'd found chair pads for the rocker in a red bandanna print. Her coffee and end tables were solid oak. She was proud of the room, proud of the whole place, for that matter. After buying the land six years ago from her earnings as a beauty operator, she'd gone into debt for the single-wide mobile home, but it would be paid for in another two years. Then she'd only have her loan for starting the business to worry about.

"We have to learn to control some of our urges for instant gratification, Gretchen," she lectured the dog as she flicked the dead bolt into place and turned out the living room lights. "If you scratch that itch without thinking, you may live to regret it."

Guiltily she remembered an urge she'd had tonight, one she'd scarcely been willing to admit to herself. When she'd leaned over Gabe Escalante, with her fingers buried in the black luxury of his hair and his eyes drifting closed, she'd had the crazy desire to lean just a little farther . . . and taste those sculpted warrior's lips.

GABE SAT on a kitchen chair in Celia's small kitchen, a bath towel pinned around his shoulders. He felt slightly more rested than he had the night before. Jasper had relieved him of watching Parnell's apartment at two that morning, and he'd gone home to sleep until nearly ten. Then he'd called Celia and talked her into finishing his haircut. But first he'd had to tell her why he needed her services, and she'd had a fit.

"I shouldn't be doing this," she muttered as she snipped at his hair. "If you're going to act like an idiot you may as well look like one."

"How do you know I'm not right? Parnell could have bought her off, couldn't he?"

"No. You weren't at the trial or you'd realize what an imbecilic thing it was to accuse that woman of something illegal. She's not the type. Now hold still."

"You should have seen how Parnell talked to her, calling her by her first name. And sending roses. What do you think of that?"

Celia combed a lock of hair away from his ear. "He does that sort of thing with women all the time. He sent me roses before I even knew who he was. That's how he operates. It means nothing."

"So you say." He noticed that Celia's scissors squeaked like an agitated mouse. Dallas's scissors had been well oiled and silent.

"Listen, Gabe, you went off half-cocked, like you tend to do when you haven't had enough sleep and you're upset. I wish you'd have told me you planned to follow Neal around. Instead you just headed out from the courthouse like some crazed version of Charles Bronson."

"I had to do something, Cel."

She waved the scissors dangerously close to his nose. "So you marched into Rowdy Ranch and insulted the foreperson of the jury."

"Who let that scumbag walk!"

Celia sighed and continued clipping. "I tried to prepare you for this, but you were so sure they'd accept my testimony. If anybody's to blame for Neal Parnell getting off, it's me."

Gabe shifted in his chair. He hated having to think about what had happened to her. It made him want to close his fingers around Parnell's throat and squeeze until all the life left his worthless body.

"Be still, Gabe, unless you want to end up looking like the lead singer in a heavy metal band."

"I don't like you blaming yourself. You reacted instinctively."

"And destroyed evidence. The prosecuting attorney told me from the beginning it would be hard to prove."

"But Dallas is a woman!"

"Hold still, Gabe!"

He quieted himself with effort. "She's a woman," he repeated more calmly. "She should have listened to your testimony and known you were telling the truth."

"When Neal had an alibi? When I'd showered away all the evidence before I worked up the courage to report it? When he wore a ski mask so I couldn't see his face? When I'm a divorced woman who dated several different men during the time I went out with Neal? You're in law enforcement, Gabe. Be realistic."

"I still say she knew him before and she swayed the jury so he'd be sure and get off."

Celia laid down the scissors and took his face in both hands. She leaned down so her dark eyes looked directly into his. "I know you're hurting, but don't strike out at someone who doesn't deserve it."

He grasped her wrists. "I want to kill him, Cel."

Fear leaped into her eyes. "No, Gabe. Please don't talk like that. You'd be the first person they'd come after if something happened to him."

He took a deep breath. "That's the only argument that's kept me from wringing his lousy neck. I won't be any help to you in jail or on the run. I won't add to what you've been through."

"Thank you."

"But I'm going to get that guy. I don't care how long it takes. I'm going to get him."

"And you're going to apologize to the jury foreperson?"

"Uh . . ."

"Gabe Escalante! What would our mother and father have said if they were still around to say it? They taught you to be a gentleman, to treat others as you would like to be treated."

"But I still don't know that she didn't—"

"I do!" She shook him gently. "And so do you, if you think about it." She smiled. "I realize apologies aren't your long suit, but you really acted like a jerk. You owe it to her. Now promise me, or I won't finish this haircut."

"Hey, Cel, give me a break."

"Promise me."

He sighed. "Okay."

3

SATURDAY NIGHT when Dallas arrived at the shop she changed the water in the flower vase and made a new diagonal cut on the stem of each rose. Then she placed the arrangement in the front of the shop, just so Gabe Escalante wouldn't miss it if he happened to come back. Not that she expected him to. And she'd certainly prefer that he didn't.

She wondered what he'd done about his unfinished haircut. Served him right. She'd saved the money he'd insolently flung on the counter and had placed it in an envelope. If he showed up at Rowdy Ranch, she'd get one of the waitresses to deliver it to him. There would be much satisfaction in doing that, but, of course, if he didn't show up, so much the better. She never wanted to see that chiseled warrior face again.

An overflow crowd kept the hair salon busy. Amber had recently started offering manicures, which had become surprisingly popular, so both women worked nearly nonstop for the first three hours they were open.

Finally there was a lull and Amber slipped out to grab a cup of coffee while Dallas took a quick inventory of supplies for her regular run to the beauty supply store on Monday. She was finishing the list when Neal Parnell walked in.

"The roses are looking good," he said with a sly wink. He wore a bright orange shirt patterned with cattle brands, and a rattlesnake hatband on his Stetson.

"They're very nice." She tucked the supply list in her pocket and hoped she was wrong about what was coming next. He took off his hat and hung it on the rack at the front of the store. Her stomach clenched.

"Thought I'd get myself a haircut."

She was trapped. Amber was taking a well-deserved break, and besides, Amber wouldn't be happy if Dallas passed Neal along to her. She forced a smile. "Fine. Have a seat."

He took the chair as if it were a throne, leaned back and closed his eyes. "I checked out the routine here. I want the works, whatever it costs."

"I give all my customers the same service."

He chuckled and opened his eyes. "That's not what I hear. The word is you threw some dude out of here last night when he was only half-done. I wouldn't want that happening to me. I like to finish what I start."

"He was rude." Dallas picked up the massage wand. "I'm sure you wouldn't be rude."

"That's right. During the trial, did I ever lose my temper? Did I ever say anything terrible?"

"No." She snapped on the wand and eased it across his shoulders.

"Ah, that feels real good, Dallas."

"It's meant to relax you."

"I'm already relaxed, sweetheart. You're the one who seems uptight."

And she was. She worked with the public nearly every day and she'd learned to accept all types of people. Nearly everyone had some characteristic she could relate to, something that would provide enough common ground to last the space of a shampoo and haircut. But with Neal she didn't even want to try.

She recalled her own words to Amber, protesting that Neal deserved to be treated like anyone else. She resolved to live by her belief. "How's the car-sales business?" she asked, pumping cheer into her voice.

"I don't want to talk about car sales, sweet thing. I want to talk about you and me."

Dallas's jaw tightened. This wouldn't be easy, but she'd handled persistent men before. She laughed as she turned the chair to face the mirror and shook out the cape. "Neal, we wouldn't get along at all. You said it yourself. I'm a workaholic. Always will be. You like to party. Besides, I'm almost thirty—too old for you."

"I prefer older women. They know the ropes."

"Well, this older woman is not a possibility for you," she said and adjusted the chair backward toward the shampoo bowl. As she tucked a towel under his neck, he grinned up at her.

"You're playing hard to get. That can be lots of fun. Just don't run away too fast."

"You completely misunderstand me," she said, and turned on the water with more force than necessary. As she worked the shampoo through his dampened brown hair, he angled his elbow so she had to work to avoid brushing her leg against it. She'd encountered that maneuver, too, but not so much recently. Usually the signals she sent out were received and her customers enjoyed the experience without pushing for more than she offered.

"You have wonderful hands, Dallas," he said.

She didn't reply, but some instinct made her glance out the front of the shop into the dance complex. There at one of the nearby pool tables stood Gabe Escalante.

Even though he wore a hat, she could tell that the sides of his hair had been evened by someone. The job didn't look quite up to her standards, but it was passable. His brown plaid shirt with the sleeves rolled back looked like a twin of the one he'd worn the day before. She could still remember how the soft material yielded as she'd moved the massage wand over the tight muscles of his back.

He held a cue stick in one hand, and his hair-sprinkled forearm flexed as he tightened his grip. He glanced with disdain at Neal reclining in the chair. When his gaze returned to her, his uncompromising expression told her exactly what he was thinking. She lifted her chin defiantly, and he turned away.

"Dallas, you're not paying attention to your customer," Neal complained.

She looked down at her hands and realized she'd stopped lathering his hair. She finished up quickly and rinsed the soap away.

GABE HAD FIGURED Parnell would return to Rowdy Ranch tonight. The punk had dragged along a couple of his drinking buddies this time, both of whom had been carded at the door. Gabe wasn't surprised that Parnell' friends were younger than he was. They were obviously his lackeys, impressionable kids who were susceptible to a guy with money to throw around.

Parnell had danced a little and had a couple of beers while he watched Dallas and Amber in the shop. When Amber had left, Parnell had started over. Gabe had decided he could use a game of pool. And there was the matter of an apology. He might as well get the damn thing over with once Parnell left the shop.

He hadn't counted on having such a visceral reaction when Dallas began running her lathered hands through Parnell's hair. Gabe didn't want her touching that piece of slime. It took all his self-control not to go in and drag Parnell from the chair, or better yet, drown him slowly in the shampoo bowl—although drowning was too good for him. As Gabe had followed the bastard around the past two days, he'd amused himself by dreaming up all sorts of exquisite tortures designed to punish a rapist.

But he could do nothing now—except maybe get the six ball in the side pocket. He was lining up the shot when someone tapped him on the shoulder. He glanced around and saw a man with a full gray beard eyeing him none too graciously. Gabe straightened.

"I don't know what's going on around here," the man said, "but I don't much like it when my friend Dallas has to put up with scum."

Gabe braced his cue stick on the carpet and leaned against it. "And?"

"She told me what you accused her of last night."

Then Gabe remembered who the guy was. "You're the photographer."

"I've known Dallas for better than a year, and you won't find a straighter shooter than she is. I don't think much of that Parnell fellow, either, but if Dallas believes he's innocent, then I believe he's innocent. And I won't have you or anybody else tarnishing her good name."

"I appreciate that, Mr. —?"

"Fogarty, Dave Fogarty."

Gabe held out his hand. "Gabe Escalante."

Fogarty hesitated, then shook his hand with obvious reluctance. "I meant what I said, Escalante."

Sizing up Fogarty and digesting his loyalty to Dallas, Gabe was beginning to see just how wrong he'd been about her. His gut had told him she was okay, but he'd ignored his instincts—always a mistake—and jumped to some stupid conclusion. Celia had been right. He'd gone off half-cocked. "Well, I plan to apologize to Dallas tonight for what I said."

A gleam appeared in Dave Fogarty's eyes. "Do you? I'm glad you told me that. Should be fun watching."

Gabe glanced uneasily at the hair salon. "Why is that?"

"If you knew Dallas better you'd understand just how deep you cut with that accusation. I'm not sure a simple apology will do the trick, but it'll be entertaining to watch you try."

Gabe groaned inwardly.

"I also have to ask myself why you seem to be around whenever this Parnell shows up. You following him or something?"

"You might say that."

Fogarty's gaze narrowed. "Are you one of those guys that takes the law into his own hands?"

"No. I just want to keep an eye on him. You and Dallas can believe he's innocent if you want, but I don't."

"Why do you care?"

Gabe forced himself to remain casual. "Let's just say I'm a concerned citizen."

"And you're not such a bad pool player, either," Fogarty said, his tone reflecting grudging respect. "I've been watching you."

Gabe noticed the photography studio hadn't yet attracted any customers, and Parnell's haircut was still in progress. "Looks like you don't have any business at the moment, and I have some time to kill before I can make that apology. Care to play?"

Fogarty studied him, obviously weighing the advisability of consorting with someone Dallas had thrown out of her shop. Finally he made up his mind. "Don't mind if I do," he said, and pulled a cue stick from the rack.

WHILE DALLAS TRIMMED Neal's hair he kept her engaged in small talk, mostly centering around how many pounds he could lift at the gym compared to his friends and how many beers he could drink in a night and still beat everybody at pool. She made appropriate admiring remarks while she watched from the corner of her eye as Dave Fogarty approached Gabe.

She could imagine the conversation from Dave's stance and the belligerent tilt of his hat. Gabe stood his ground, too, and Dallas hoped they wouldn't start swinging. Dave was at least fifteen years older and thirty pounds lighter than Gabe. Gabe's poise in the face of a challenge told Dallas that he was used to winning physical confrontations.

When Gabe held out his hand to Dave, Dallas nearly poked Neal in the eye with the scissors.

"Watch it, hon!" Neal said.

"I'm sorry." She focused more intently on her task. She'd never injured a customer yet, and now wasn't the time to start, especially with someone like Neal who would probably sue for all she owned. But why were those two men *shaking hands*?

"I need my baby blues, you know," Neal said.

"I promise it won't happen again." She thought "baby blues" was a perfect description for Neal's eyes. In fact, his whole face had a childlike softness. Although by traditional standards he'd be called handsome, Dallas preferred a face with a more lived-in look. A face like . . . Gabe's. But Gabe was a jerk.

And when next she looked, the jerk was playing pool with Dave. Apparently defending her honor had become less important to Dave than a challenging game of pool. Men.

She completed Neal's haircut and put in a few finishing touches with a comb and blow dryer while Neal gazed at himself admiringly.

"You have the touch," he said. "As of now I'm yours for life."

Dallas controlled her expression and managed a smile as she unsnapped his cape. "I'm glad you like it."

Neal stood and reached for his wallet. "I'll show you how much I like it." He handed her a hundred-dollar bill. "Keep the change."

"Neal, this is far too much for—"

He closed her hand around the money. "There's more where that came from. Listen, if you're nervous about seeing me here in town, we could go away for a couple of days. Let me take you to Vegas, or La Jolla. Hell, San Francisco's a plane ride away. How about it?"

Dallas withdrew her hand. She'd been able to dismiss this sort of overture easily before. But Neal was different. Rejecting him seemed like a form of discrimination, as if she considered him tainted just by being accused of a crime. She didn't believe that was right. But she didn't want to go out with him, either.

"I can see you're thinking about it."

"No, not really. Listen, it's not the trial, Neal. I just don't think we're right for each other."

"Oh, yes, you do. You watched me during the trial, and I could tell how you felt about me. Give in to your fantasies, Dallas." He lowered his voice. "Let yourself go, baby. I can make it good for you, better than you've ever had it."

Appalled by his audacity, Dallas backed up a step. "I'm sorry, but our relationship will have to remain as customer and client."

"What's the matter, got a boyfriend?"

"No." She should have said she had, but she hated lying, no matter what the circumstances.

Neal grinned. "A girlfriend?"

"No!"

"Because I wouldn't care if you did. Might make things more interesting."

"If you'll excuse me, I have work to do." She tucked the money in her pocket and reached for the broom.

He wagged a finger in her face. "You're avoiding me, and that's not nice. But I'm stubborn, and I'm not giving up yet."

She stared at him. Was this spoiled rich boy so lonely that he'd hang around waiting for her to change her mind? "I'm sure there are lots of women here at Rowdy Ranch who would be delighted to spend their evenings with you. Why waste time on a lost cause?"

"You're not a lost cause, and you're the one I want," he said, and plucked his hat from the rack. "See you around, sweet thing."

Dallas shook her head in wonder as he headed for a table full of people and clapped a young man on the back. The man, who looked barely twenty-one, handed over his beer and Neal tipped his head back and chugalugged it. Dallas looked more closely at the friend and realized he was the one who'd been Neal's alibi for the night Celia Martinez claimed she was raped. As Dallas watched, another young man passed his beer to Neal, who drained that glass, too. Then he signaled for a waitress.

"He's a real piece of work."

She glanced to her left and found Gabe standing near the entrance to the shop, watching her. Her back stiffened. "I believe we've had this conversation." She turned away and began sweeping.

"We need to have it again."

She whirled back to him. He'd stepped inside. "I don't recall inviting you in to chat."

"We need to iron out some things, Dallas."

"*We* don't need to do anything. *You* need to leave, unless you want me to call security and have you thrown out." She quickly calculated whether Frank and Turner, the bouncers on duty, could handle somebody like Gabe. She wasn't convinced they could, but he didn't have to know that.

"I'm not leaving until we get a few things straight."

She hung the broom on its hook and glared at him. "That imperious air won't work with me, Mr. Escalante. I'm not easily intimidated. Shall I call security, or will you leave quietly?"

He rubbed the back of his neck. "Dammit, Fogarty was right about you."

"Excuse me?"

"He said you might not accept a simple apology."

Her mouth dropped open. "A simple *what?*"

Gabe glanced away. "Apology," he said, as if forcing the word past his lips.

"That's what you've been doing?" She began to laugh. "You call ordering me to talk with you an apology?"

He stuffed his hands in his back pockets and gazed up at the ceiling. "If I can't talk with you, how can I tell you that I might have been a little out of line last night?"

"A *little* out of line?" She folded her arms across her chest and narrowed her eyes. "You mean you're reconsidering the idea that I have the hots for Neal Parnell, or worse yet, took a bribe from him?"

He met her gaze. "That's right."

Too bad he looked so magnificent standing there, but she had her principles. "I'm truly touched."

"You have to admit it looked bad, with him coming in here the same day as the trial ended, calling you by your first name, giving you flowers."

"I don't have to admit a damned thing, Mr. Escalante. My conscience is clear, but I hope yours is really bothering you, because what you did was arrogant, judgmental and exceedingly rude."

The muscles in his jaw tightened. "Now wait a minute. Considering Parnell's reputation, I had every right to—"

"You had no right, and you've run out of time for this so-called apology, mister." She turned and picked up the envelope containing his payment for the haircut. Taking one step forward, she extended the envelope. "Here's the money you gave me last night. I refuse to accept payment for a job I didn't finish. Take it and leave."

He made no movement toward the envelope as he gazed at her. "You took Parnell's money."

"Of course." A shiver of awareness passed through her as she realized how closely he must have been watching her with those dark, compelling eyes. "I finished that job." But she'd had a tough time with Neal's haircut, especially with Gabe hovering nearby. She resented the unsettling effect Gabe had on her.

"Dallas, he's a dangerous man."

She braced her hands on her hips. "What are you, the king of the world? A modern-day version of Sigmund Freud or Solomon? What gives you the authority to pass that kind of judgment?"

He sighed. "I'm a bail-enforcement officer."

She paused and turned the label over in her mind. "You mean a bounty hunter?"

"If you insist, yes."

"Is there a bounty on Neal's head?"

"No, but he's bad news. Over the years I've learned to read people and—"

"Oh, I see. And you're so good at reading people that you just knew I was the sort to rig a trial, right?" She rolled her eyes. "Boy, am I impressed with your insights, Mr. Bounty Hunter."

"I was tired. I wasn't thinking straight."

"That's for darned sure."

"Listen, your opinion of me doesn't matter, but stay away from Parnell. Get your security guys to escort him out of your shop next time. Make sure someone walks you to the parking lot every night. Reinforce the locks on your doors and windows at home."

"First a bogus apology, now scare tactics. I can take care of myself, thank you. And Neal is a mixed-up young man, but he's not a criminal. Go chase somebody else." She waved the envelope at him. "Here's your money."

"I don't want it," he said quietly. "And you need to take me seriously about Parnell. I'll be around, if you want to discuss it some more."

"What are you going to do, watch over me?"

He regarded her steadily. "Yes."

Unexpected warmth cascaded over her, and she maintained her defiant pose with effort. "That's ridiculous."

"Not if Parnell's picked you as his next victim." Gabe turned and walked out of the shop.

4

MINUTES AFTER GABE LEFT the shop, Dave Fogarty showed up, looking sheepish.

Dallas glared at him. "I thought you offered to protect me from him."

"Well, I talked with the guy and—" He shrugged. "He seems okay."

"He plays a good game of pool, is what you mean to say."

"Now, Dallas, it's not just that. I put a lot of store by a person's handshake, and if they look me in the eye when I meet them." Dave scratched his beard. "Didn't seem like you accepted his apology."

Dallas's laugh was short and harsh. "That man wouldn't know an apology if it bit him in the backside."

"I figured as much. But I think he's okay. Don't know what his deal is with Parnell, though."

"Let me tell you." Dallas lined up the bottles of shampoo and conditioner more precisely on the shelf behind the shampoo bowl. "Mr. Escalante should have been born a hundred years ago, when differences of opinion were settled at high noon in some dusty cowtown street. He's trying to create drama where there is none, because he's bored with the civilized life the rest of us enjoy. Did you know he's a bounty hunter?"

Dave's eyes widened. "No, I didn't."

"My guess is he's between jobs right now and needs something to occupy his time. Go ahead and play pool with him if you want, Dave, but I sure wouldn't take anything he says seriously."

Dave glanced back at the bar where Gabe was sitting with his hand wrapped around a mug of beer. "A bounty hunter, huh? I didn't think they existed anymore."

"He calls himself a bail-enforcement officer." Dallas's voice slid mockingly over the description. "I think he has an exaggerated idea of his importance in this world."

Dave returned his attention to Dallas. "I hope it won't bother you if I play pool with him now and then. He can really shoot out the lights with that stick."

Dallas shook her head. Apparently men were more easily fooled by macho swagger than women. "No, I don't care, Dave. Just so I don't have to deal with him anymore."

DURING THE NEXT WEEK, Dallas wondered if Neal realized he had a shadow. Every time he came into Rowdy Ranch, she had only to look around a few minutes later to see Gabe at the bar or choosing a cue stick at the pool tables near her shop. But other people came into the dance hall every night, so maybe Neal hadn't taken notice of Gabe.

Dallas wished she could ignore him, too, but his presence unsettled her more than she cared to admit. Apparently she wasn't the only woman who experienced a rush of adrenaline whenever Gabe showed up.

He began getting dance requests, and eventually he accepted a few. When he was on the floor with someone in his arms, Dallas battled an underlying agitation that made no sense. Why should she care if he danced, and with whom? But she found herself judging each partner's attractiveness and skill. Even Amber noticed her preoccupation, and Dallas had to do some fast talking to convince Amber she wasn't interested in Gabe.

During the evening she tried not to leave herself open to advances from Neal, but he caught her on Thursday night when she stopped by the bar for a glass of soda.

"Taking a break, sweet thing?" He leaned against the bar, nearly touching her.

She shifted away from him. "Just getting something to drink."

"How about a dance?" He glanced toward the shop. "Nobody's waiting for one of your famous haircuts right now."

She grabbed the cold glass that the bartender handed her. "Thanks, anyway, but I'm expecting a customer any minute," she said, starting away from the bar.

"Is that right?" Neal caught her arm and she flinched. "I'd hate to think you were telling old Neal a story."

She glanced back at him and eased her arm from his grip. "I work for a living," she said with more acidity than she'd intended. But he was restricting her freedom of movement, and she didn't like it. "I can't go running off whenever I get the urge."

"And are you getting the urge?" he asked with a smile.

"Excuse me. I have to get back." She turned and hurried toward the shop, but her way was blocked by her other nemesis, who stepped away from the pool table and into her path.

"You'd better think about what I said. Parnell's becoming more persistent," Gabe said, studying her.

"I'd say you both hold the world's record for that trait."

"Don't let anger make you careless." The rough timbre of his voice and the intensity in his eyes stopped her from walking away.

She swallowed. "I can handle him."

"In here, maybe. But out there? Don't kid yourself." His glance moved over her. "And that outfit doesn't help your cause, either. You must know you're dressed like every cowboy's dream."

Against her will her body responded with a warm flush.

"Now it's real nice for those of us with some restraint," he continued, "but tempting a man like Parnell with tight little shorts is dangerous."

"I beg your pardon!" she exclaimed, glad for an excuse to be angry. "What I wear is none of your concern!"

"I'm only trying to warn you."

"Save it." She pushed past him and stormed into her shop, her heart beating wildly. Once again he'd completely destroyed her composure. What right did he have making such personal comments about her appearance? Some nerve, to discuss her tight shorts. *Which means he's noticed*, whispered her libido. *And you like that, don't you?* Desire, so carefully monitored and controlled, began stretching within her. She didn't want to feel this craving for Gabe Escalante, but apparently she couldn't help herself.

As the minutes ticked away, she was aware of every move he made over by the pool tables. And with that awareness, passion shouldered its way to the forefront of her consciousness. She'd never paid much attention to the lyrics of the country songs played at Rowdy Ranch, but tonight the words of love and lust wouldn't leave her alone. *I want you*, crooned a song, and instinctively Dallas glanced over at the pool tables.

As if sensing the direction of her gaze, he looked up. She turned away, not ready to confront that heated stare. Moments later, she found herself watching him again, and again he lifted his head from the shot he'd been about to make. This time she didn't look away. *Love me tonight*, demanded another song. *Love me now. Love me right.* She noticed Gabe's fingers tighten on the pool cue and saw a muscle twitch in his jaw. Longing exploded within Dallas and she trembled. Her customer spoke to her, and with an effort she broke the charged connection with Gabe.

She forced herself to concentrate on her work, until a familiar phrase from a new song distracted her again. Something about "a cowboy's dream." That's what Gabe had called her. She'd been unable to forget the way he'd looked at her when he'd said it, as if he wanted to take her in his arms and kiss her senseless. She'd reacted to his comments with anger because she couldn't allow him to see that he'd touched a deep chord of sensuality that was still vibrating.

She tried to ignore the song, but the words hammered at her. *And I'm going crazy, no matter how cool*

I seem, 'cause she is the answer to this cowboy's dream.
Dallas clenched her jaw. She wouldn't look at Gabe.
She wouldn't. But at last she peeked in the direction of
the pool tables. He wasn't there. Disappointment felt
like a soggy lump in her stomach.

Wondering if he'd left for the night, she glanced out
toward the bar. He sat on a stool, a half-empty mug of
beer in one hand, his gaze fastened on her.

The song's refrain swirled between them—*'cause she
is the answer to this cowboy's dream.* Dallas's heartbeat quickened as he slowly raised the mug in salute.
Then he winked, tilted back his head and drained the
contents of the mug. When she returned to her haircut,
her hands quivered so much she almost snipped off the
tip of her customer's ear.

THE NEXT MORNING Dallas made a long-overdue phone
call across town to her mother. She hoped Lucille Frakes
had found a job. When she and Dallas's stepfather had
decided to relocate from Texas to Arizona, Dallas had
thought she'd be able to convince her mother to find
work. Lucille was far too dependent on Jeb Frakes for
Dallas's taste, but then her mother had always allowed
men, including Dallas's father, to dominate her.

After answering the phone and sounding delighted
to talk, Lucille chattered in southern-belle style about
the activities of Dallas's two brothers, two sisters and
their respective offspring. Dallas listened patiently until her mother wound down.

"Any luck with a job?" she asked finally.

There was a pause. "Well, you know that Jeb prefers I not work." Lucille sounded as if she were sitting on a veranda sipping mint juleps and supervising the help.

But Dallas knew they didn't have much money, and Jeb was making very little as a clerk in an auto-parts store. "Mom, I don't think—"

"Dallas, you're not married, and you don't know about these things. Most men's egos can't stand up to a woman bringing in money of her own. I tried that with your father, and you see what happened."

Dallas wanted to scream, but even screaming wouldn't change the way her mother looked at life. Deserted by one weak man when Dallas was sixteen, Lucille had promptly found another whose self-esteem fed on denying any to his wife. Dallas had moved away from Amarillo partly to free herself from her stepfather's dictatorial ways. But ten years had passed, and Dallas foolishly had dreamed that she could influence her mother to lead a more productive existence than catering to the whims of a middle-aged man.

Apparently that wouldn't happen. Dallas took a deep breath. "If men are all that sensitive, then I'd rather not have one around."

Her mother's chuckle lacked humor. "You may not have to worry. You plum scare men off, Dallas. I've told you that before."

"Maybe I just scare off the wrong ones. Maybe the right one wouldn't be scared at all."

"If there is such a man," her mother said. "You're such an idealist."

Dallas gripped the phone. "I'll tell you this. I'd rather live alone all my life than be tied to someone who tells me what to do."

"They all try, honey." Her mother's sigh, heavy with resignation, drifted across the telephone line. "They all try."

THE TENSION BUILT between Gabe and Dallas each night at Rowdy Ranch. Dallas suspected that without Neal in the picture, they might have acted on their obvious attraction to each other. But Gabe's hostility toward Neal stood between them.

During the day Dallas distracted herself with the routine she loved—taking long horseback rides into the Tucson Mountain foothills, making improvements to her property and having an occasional lunch and shopping trip with Amber.

The weather continued unseasonably warm for February, which brought more than the usual flock of winter visitors to Tucson. Cadillacs and Lincolns with out-of-state plates clogged the roads as Dallas drove into town one sunny morning to pick up dog food.

The influx of tourists would bring more business to Rowdy Ranch, she reasoned. The idea cheered her and she began singing along with Alan Jackson's "Chattahoochee" on the radio. She swung into the parking lot of the pet store to pick up the special brand of dog food she fed Gretchen. She'd be glad when Gretchen wasn't in season anymore. Usually she brought the Great Dane along on shopping trips and left her guarding the truck. But Gretchen couldn't socialize again until she stopped panting after every male dog within a square-mile radius.

Inside the pet store she wasted no time. She still had a list of projects for the day, including putting another coat of paint on the tack shed. She'd just hefted a twenty-pound bag of chow into her cart when Neal Parnell sauntered down the aisle, grinning at her.

GABE HAD STAYED with Parnell until nearly five in the morning. Parnell and his buddies had closed down Rowdy Ranch at two before heading out into the desert to drink beer they'd bought at a convenience store. Gabe had followed at a safe distance and parked off the road about a half mile from the spot where Neal and his friends partied around a makeshift fire of mesquite and creosote. The pungent odor of the burning wood and the loud voices didn't draw the attention of any passing patrol cars. Gabe had hoped they would, so he could go home to bed, but no such luck.

Parnell seemed to be drinking more recently and spending fewer hours at the dealership. Jasper and Diego's reports indicated he put in less than two hours at work each day. Gabe figured the wilder Parnell became, the greater the chance he'd tip his hand by molesting another woman. His continued attentions to Dallas told Gabe who that woman was likely to be.

A little before 5:00 a.m. the party finally broke up and Gabe followed Parnell back to his apartment before putting in a call to Diego to spell him. He felt lucky both Diego and Jasper were available. If a more lucrative job came along, either of them might be forced to take it, but for now they were unemployed and willing to help out for a modest fee.

Once Diego arrived, Gabe drove home and fell into bed with his clothes on. Something would break soon, he thought, just before sleep claimed him.

The phone woke him and he reached for it with the automatic reflex of someone used to interrupted sleep.

Diego spoke without preamble. "He's found out where she lives, amigo. I followed him to the turnoff to her house. He waited behind some bushes until she drove away, then tailed her into town and went into the pet store after she did. They came out together, arguing. It looked like he wanted to carry her dog food and she wouldn't let him."

Gabe rubbed one eye with the heel of his hand. He'd been right. The campaign was escalating. Maybe Dallas would realize that now. "What happened after that?" he asked.

"She drove away, and I guess he was ticked, because he peeled out and tore over to the grocery store *muy pronto* to buy some beer before he went home. He's still in his apartment, probably polishing off the six-pack. Thought you'd want the update."

"*Si. Gracias*, amigo. Stay there until I can grab a shower and call Jasper. I want to take it from here today."

"Want some help?"

"Not yet, but maybe soon. *Adios*." The excitement of the chase banished his tiredness. It always did.

DALLAS HOPED THAT AFTER the argument in the parking lot of the pet store and Neal's abrupt exit she'd be rid of him for good. But that night, when he showed up at Rowdy Ranch, that hope died.

"You women's-lib types are making a mistake," he said, leaning in the doorway of her shop while she was finishing a trim on a customer. "If you don't let us help out once in a while, we're liable to quit offering."

"Hello, Neal," she said. "You'll have to excuse me. I'm busy with a client just now."

"Yeah, okay." He pushed away from the doorway. "Just wanted to mention a mutual acquaintance we have, Stewart Ellison. The Ellisons lived next to us when I was growing up. I understand you know him, too. Small world, huh?"

Dread touched the small of her back with icy fingers. Stewart Ellison held her business loan. Was Neal threatening to have that loan called in? "Yes, I do business with Mr. Ellison," she said, not looking at Neal.

"Well, like I said, he's a good friend of the family's. Thought you'd want to know."

She looked up, trying to gauge the level of menace in his statement. She didn't like the speculative expression on his face.

"See you around, sweet thing." He turned on his expensively booted heel and swaggered away.

"Sounds like he's trying to make an impression on you," the customer said.

"I guess he is." Dallas unclenched her teeth and willed herself to relax. Maybe that was all Neal meant, after all. He just wanted to let her know he had important friends. "That takes care of you for another couple of weeks, Mr. Nelson." She unsnapped the cape and removed it before handing him a mirror.

"Somebody should tell that poor boy he has the wrong approach." He held the mirror and admired the back of his head. "Nice job, as usual, Dallas."

"Thank you." She accepted his payment and smiled her goodbyes, although a piercing headache had lodged just behind her right eye. Neal was getting very tiresome. She heard loud laughter and glanced out the door in time to see Neal hugging Beth, one of the waitresses. With luck he would find someone else to bother. She fervently hoped so, because she couldn't have him embarrassing her in front of customers. Maybe she would have to speak to the security staff, although she hated to make an issue of his behavior. She wished this wasn't Amber's night off. She'd like to discuss the situation with someone.

As if on cue, Gabe Escalante walked in. Definitely not the person she wanted to discuss her problem with.

He shoved his hands in the pockets of his worn jeans and cleared his throat. "There's something you need to know."

Willing her heart to stop beating so fast, she turned away and reached for the broom to sweep up. "I can just imagine."

"Parnell didn't find you at the pet supply store by accident. He followed you there from your trailer."

She whirled and stared at him, her stomach churning. "How do you know that? And how do you know I live in a trailer?"

He looked slightly uncomfortable, but he met her gaze. "I have two men on Parnell. The three of us have him covered around the clock. One of the guys followed him to your place, or at least he figured out it was your place when he saw you drive away."

Dallas backed up a step, a protective hand to her chest. "You are certifiable. What in God's name are you doing following that man twenty-four hours a day?"

"I told you. He's dangerous."

"According to you!" Dallas saw a customer coming toward the shop and lowered her voice. "Look, I don't have much experience with this sort of reckless bounty-hunter mentality, but I think it's pretty stupid. Neal could have you arrested for harrassment."

"He could." Gabe hooked his thumbs in his belt loops and gave her a hard look. "Especially if you tell him about it. I took a chance by coming in here. I had some idea you should be warned."

Dallas inclined her head toward the bar, where Neal had one arm around Beth. "Maybe you'd better warn her, too. And everyone he dances with."

Gabe followed the direction of her glance. "Might not be a bad idea. But you're the only one whose home he's staked out."

"Staked out?" She rolled her eyes. "You're giving me dialogue out of a grade-B movie. This version may not fit your sense of drama, but I'll bet he happened to drive that way and recognized my truck. Avra Valley Road is a well-traveled road."

"*And he followed you into town.* Don't you get it?"

"He has a crush. That's *all*." She turned toward her customer with a forced smile. "Mr. Abernathy! How great to see you again."

Gabe stepped closer. "Listen, Dallas—"

"I have work to do," she said in an undertone.

He strode away, obviously furious. She was surprised that he didn't leave Rowdy Ranch, but apparently he was still on his appointed mission and stayed nearby for most of the night, playing pool with Dave Fogarty. Dammit, he was getting to her, making her jumpy when there was no evidence she should be. Neal hadn't done anything wrong. He was heavy-handed, but there wasn't a law against boorishness.

That night she drove home constantly glancing in her rearview mirror, but she never spied a black Corvette or a battered old truck behind her. Once home she checked and rechecked her locks. Damn that Gabe, anyway, for frightening her. Fortunately the next night was Friday, and Amber would be working with her. For the first time, she was uneasy about being alone.

THE NEXT AFTERNOON Dallas decided to make a coffee ice-cream run. When life puttered along without incident, she didn't much care what she ate. But when the bumpy times arrived, she needed her number-one comfort food. She'd finished off a half gallon during the trial, and she needed another one.

"You could probably use a little yourself," she told Gretchen. The dog whined and wagged her thick rope of a tail. "In fact, you may be under more stress than I am. But the vet and I think it's best, Gretchen. You'll have stronger puppies if we just wait this one out, okay?"

Gretchen cocked her head and wagged her tail harder.

"I knew you'd see it my way. Be back in a flash."

Driving felt good, with the window down and the radio blaring on KIIM-FM, a Tucson country station. She took along a small cooler in which to bring back the ice cream.

On the freeway she glanced back to change lanes and saw a black car about half a mile behind her.

"I'm getting paranoid," she muttered, and turned the radio up louder.

She took the Ina Road exit. At the first stoplight she checked her rearview mirror. Sure enough. A black Corvette. She felt as if someone were playing marbles in her stomach. Maybe it wasn't Neal. There were other black Corvettes in Tucson. She turned off the radio.

By the time she reached the ice-cream store her hands were slippery on the wheel. The black car turned into the shopping center and pulled up beside her. She sat in the truck with the motor still running, her legs shaking so much she had a hard time keeping her foot on the brake pedal.

Neal was the driver of the car.

5

DALLAS WISHED she'd checked behind her earlier, when she'd pulled out on Avra Valley Road. She had no real proof that Neal had followed her from there, or that he'd parked somewhere nearby to watch her. But if he had...

He got out of the car and glanced around. Then he demonstrated great surprise when he saw her sitting in her truck. With a smile he started toward her.

Dallas didn't stop to think. She threw the truck into reverse and backed out of the parking space. By some miracle no one was behind her. She put the truck into gear and shot out away from the ice-cream store without looking back.

She drove around with no pattern, her thoughts racing, her attention constantly flicking to the rearview mirror. After fifteen minutes with no black Corvette in sight, she began to relax a little. Was she overreacting? Neal could have ended up at the same ice-cream store by coincidence, couldn't he?

She knew what the answer was, but she didn't want to face it, because facing it would mean she'd have to admit that Neal was acting in a threatening way. If he could have her business loan recalled, then taking action against him could have serious consequences. And there was the other, more disturbing question. If he was capable of harrassing her like this, was he capable of other, more sinister things?

"No," she said aloud. "He's just a mixed-up, spoiled rich boy." She glanced at her watch. Time to go home and change for work. And if Neal showed up tonight, she'd tell him to quit following her. She could handle this.

"DALLAS, I AGREE with Gabe. Neal's dangerous." Amber stood her ground as they faced each other in the shop that night. "Get some help."

Dallas gazed at Amber, the cleaning rag in her hand forgotten. While they'd been readying the shop for business she'd told Amber about the two incidents with Neal and his comment about being friends with her banker. She'd almost hoped Amber would brush them off as unimportant. "But logically he's done nothing wrong. Probably he just needs a firmer declaration from me."

"You've left no doubt about your feelings, and he hasn't given up. Stop using that damned logic of yours and pay attention to your gut. How does that feel?"

Dallas pressed a hand to her stomach. "Terrible."

"Then do something about it. Call the police."

"The police? What about my business loan? He said—"

"Your life is more important than your business. These past two meetings sound like he's turning into a stalker."

"But there's still the chance that I'm overreacting, that Gabe has me spooked and—"

"I don't think so, Dallas. Listen, if you don't feel right contacting the police, what about talking to Gabe? Dave really likes him, and I've been impressed myself. The man looks like he could handle Neal Parnell with one hand tied behind his back. He probably has some intimidation tactics of his own."

Dallas certainly believed that. But what would it cost her to deal with Gabe, a man whose mere glance in her direction caused an internal meltdown?

"Talk to him," Amber urged, squeezing Dallas's arm.

Dallas felt her options narrowing. She'd vowed not to make the first move in Gabe's direction, but Neal was scaring her and she probably needed Gabe's help. Perhaps the smoldering looks she'd exchanged with him during the past few nights meant less than she thought they did. Then again, maybe they meant that once they were alone they'd tear each other's clothes off.

No, they wouldn't. She wasn't that sort of woman. She didn't act on impulse, and her basic character wasn't about to change just because of one sexy man. She sighed. "All right. I'll talk to him."

As GABE STEPPED into the neon grotto of Rowdy Ranch Friday night he wondered if Dallas finally understood she had a problem. But he'd decided to let her come to him. Her fierce independence reminded him of the spirited mare he'd ridden years ago on the ranch. Try to chase her down and you'd never get anywhere. But if you stayed still, let her think things over, she'd sometimes come right up to you. Sometimes.

Gabe had been third in the caravan to the ice-cream store. She'd left without her ice cream, which told him she was finally getting scared. Good. She needed to be scared enough to come to him for help. So he would wait.

As the evening wore on, Gabe noticed that Parnell didn't go near the shop. Too bad, Gabe thought. He wanted the threat underlined for Dallas, so she'd have no doubt. Maybe Parnell was smarter than he'd thought. The punk spent most of his time with Beth. She wore what looked like diamond studs in her earlobes, and Parnell kept nibbling them. Gabe concluded that the sickening interplay meant Parnell had given her the earrings. If the creep didn't leave her alone, he was liable to get her fired.

The music grew louder as the crowd thickened like simmering chili. After three line dances in a row to stir things up, the disk jockey played a waltz while the mirrored ball flicked shredded light over the dancers like transparent confetti. Gabe turned down two requests to dance and challenged a college kid in a University of Arizona sweatshirt and Reebok running shoes to a game of pool. All the while he kept watching, watching.

Finally about nine-thirty he snapped the pool cue back into its holder and opted out of the next game. He couldn't wait for Dallas to come to him, after all. Parnell could easily try something tonight, and she needed to be prepared for it. He'd talk to her, whether she wanted to listen or not. He turned toward the salon and stopped abruptly. She was walking in his direction. At last.

IF AMBER HADN'T threatened to go in her place, Dallas wouldn't have followed through on her promise to talk to Gabe about Neal. After all, Neal seemed to be totally involved with Beth tonight and hadn't even made his usual passes by the salon. But Dallas knew Amber would go to Gabe if she didn't, and she preferred to keep some control over the situation by talking to him herself. She watched him from the corner of her eye, and when he hung up his cue stick she happened to be without a customer. She started toward the pool tables just as he turned toward her.

His direct gaze disconcerted her. She'd meant to approach him subtly, coming up from the side, catching him slightly unaware and maybe a little unguarded. She wondered if he was ever unguarded.

As she approached, she felt as if she were walking along an unrolled red carpet toward an audience with a prince. Perhaps the Prince of Darkness, she thought, as his brown eyes studied her with an intensity that made her shiver. He lifted his eyebrows ever so slightly in question as she drew near.

"I'd like to talk with you privately," she said.

Something flickered in his gaze. "Let's dance, then."

"Oh, I don't—"

"Don't dance? I find that hard to believe."

"No, I can dance. But I don't think dancing is necessary to our conversation."

"It's the most private place I can think of." His lips curved. "No one can overhear you if you keep moving."

"All right." Darn her silly heart, beating like crazy as he took her hand and led her to the polished wooden floor. His touch was firm, the skin on his fingers slightly chapped. She liked that work-roughened feel, had never quite trusted baby-soft hands.

A two-step was in progress, and he whirled her into his arms with practiced ease. His hand against her shoulder blade exerted just enough pressure to guide her into the rhythm. She rested her left hand lightly against his collarbone, keeping several inches between them, although he didn't try to maneuver her closer. The flannel of his shirt teased her palm with softness as he moved in time with a Clint Black song. As if they'd been partners for years, they danced unerringly around the oval floor, her bare legs brushing the denim of his jeans.

His scent reached her—a woodsy fragrance mingled with the tang of beer. His hand was warm against her back. She leaned back just a little, and he supported her. Safe. That's what she was feeling, for the first time in days.

Startled by the emotion, she glanced into his face, and the illusion shattered. She wasn't safe with this man. When she looked into his eyes her pulse leaped and her throat went dry. He'd offered to help protect her from Neal Parnell, but who would protect her from Gabe?

The music ended, but he still held her firmly in his arms. Before she could suggest they leave the floor, a waltz began. Gabe moved into the flowing rhythm as if born to it.

Dallas sighed involuntarily. She'd forgotten how much she loved to waltz. And this man knew how to do it. Long, languorous strides carried her through the dip and flow, lift and whirl. Her cares slid away as he led her smoothly, never missing a step, never allowing her to falter.

"You wanted to talk?" His breath feathered her ear.

She glanced into his knowing eyes, her lips a fraction away from his. "Not yet."

A spark kindled in his dark gaze. His grip on her shoulder tightened and his lead became more forceful. On a swell of music they soared—swooping like hawks riding the desert wind. She would give a great deal to have this go on . . . and on.

But the music ended and she gazed at him with regret. Another two-step followed, and with a slow smile he urged her gently backward in the familiar six-count movement.

"I love to waltz," she confessed, keeping her eyes focused on the curve of his shoulder.

"So do I." His deep voice, so close, drew a tremor of reaction from her.

"I suppose you know Neal followed me to the ice-cream store today."

"I know."

"I'm not admitting he's anything more than a nuisance."

"That's your privilege, although you're wrong."

She took a steadying breath. "Maybe we shouldn't have this conversation." She shifted as if to move out of his arms.

"Stay." His grip tightened slightly, but she could feel the restrained power and knew that if he really wanted to hold her there she'd be unable to get away. "Please."

She glanced up at him. "What's your stake in this?"

"I told you. I don't like to see slime like Parnell get away with intimidating women." The lines of anger bracketing his mouth made him look capable of avenging all the wrongs of the world.

"Well, Amber told me I should get some help."

The angry lines softened, and he looked down, deliberately capturing her gaze. "Here I am."

She had trouble breathing. *Here I am.* Three simple words. Ah, but how they complicated her life. This rough, tough bounty hunter scared her to death. She didn't want to need him, didn't want to need anyone, but it seemed at the moment she had no choice. "What—" She stumbled over the question, hating to ask it of anyone, least of all this man. "What do you think I should do?"

"For starters, let me check the security on your trailer."

"My locks are fine."

"I'd like to make sure."

Well, she'd asked for his help, and she wasn't an expert on locks. In his line of work, he probably had to be. "When?"

"Tonight, if possible."

She hesitated. Maybe Dave liked his handshake and Amber liked his buns, but Dallas didn't know Gabe well enough to be alone at night in an isolated trailer with him.

As if reading her thoughts, he spoke. "I can give you the numbers of two bail bondsmen I've worked for. They'll vouch for me."

"Tonight?"

Gabe chuckled. "They call me at all hours. Besides, they're both night people. They'll be up."

"All right. I'll call." And if he checked out okay, which she guessed he would, she would be alone tonight with this man who made her skin tingle wherever he touched, who made her completely forget herself as she whirled in his arms on a crowded dance floor. What would happen when they closed the door on the world?

Nothing. This man was too hot to handle. If she ever gave up a small measure of her independence to someone, it wouldn't be some vigilante type who thrived on drama and danger. She wiped all emotion from her face before she met his eyes again. "I'll let you know when I've contacted your references." She could tell by the slight falter in his gaze that he'd noticed her subtle rejection. His expression closed down.

At that moment Neal tapped on Gabe's shoulder. "My turn, buddy."

Gabe glanced over his shoulder and Dallas felt him stiffen, but he didn't interrupt his rhythm. "No."

Neal shoved a pair of dancers aside and followed. "Hey, I—"

"Sorry." Gabe ground out his denial as he placed himself between Neal and Dallas. In seconds they'd danced away from where Neal stood, face distorted with fury.

Dallas gratefully accepted the mantle of Gabe's protection as it settled over her. Like a fool she'd imagined Neal's obsession with her had ended, but she'd been wrong. Everything Gabe had predicted so far had turned out to be true. And Gabe thought Neal was a rapist. Dallas turned away from the thought. Gabe hadn't heard the testimony, and he, like most people, was ready to believe the worst of someone like Neal.

Still, she was very glad Gabe hadn't allowed Neal to cut in. "Thank you," she murmured.

"Anytime." His tone had become impersonal and instead of holding her gaze, he glanced toward the hair salon. "I don't know if you've noticed, but Amber's up to her eyebrows over there. Two guys are waiting, and a third just walked up."

Chagrined, Dallas broke away from the circle of his arms. "My God, I never take this long a break."

He caught her arm as she started from the dance floor. "Let me give you those numbers."

"Oh. Of course." With the way he'd championed her on the dance floor she felt less need for references, but checking them would be the prudent thing to do. She waited while he pulled a card and a pencil stub from his back pocket and scribbled on the back before handing it to her.

"Thanks," she said, taking the card. It was curved, pressed that way by the shape of his buttocks, and still warm. She made the mistake of glancing into his eyes, and a potent image of making love to Gabe hit with a force that took her breath away. "I'd better go," she managed in a breathy whisper and nearly ran toward the salon.

Suddenly Neal blocked her way. "Why did you tear off like that today? I was ready to buy you an ice-cream cone."

"Neal, I—"

Gabe's abrupt appearance cut off her reply. He stepped in front of her and faced Neal. "The lady has work to do."

Neal sneered. "You her boyfriend or something?"

"Yes."

"She said she didn't have one."

"I guess she and I will have to talk about that." Gabe reached for Dallas and guided her gently toward the salon. "Go ahead. I'll take care of this."

"Gabe, maybe—"

"I can deal with him. Go."

PARNELL'S EYES GLITTERED as he faced Gabe. "You can't tell me who I can talk to and who I can't, cowboy."

"You were keeping her from her customers." Gabe clenched his hands at his sides. If Parnell provoked him into a fight, they could both end up being escorted from the place in a squad car. He'd love to see it happen to Parnell, but the jerk could probably post bail quicker than he could, and Dallas might be in danger.

Parnell hitched his belt up a notch. "Well, I'm a pretty good customer myself, if you know what I mean."

His smirk nearly tempted Gabe into throwing a punch. "Don't push it, Parnell."

"Oh, you know who I am?"

"Unfortunately."

Parnell looked him up and down. "Well, I could buy and sell you, buddy. You don't have a chance with me around."

It took all of Gabe's control not to strangle him on the spot. "We'll see about that." Then he turned his back and walked away.

God, he wanted a beer, but now was not the time. He needed a clear head for the next few hours. Alcohol might lower his resistance to Dallas, and despite what he'd said to Parnell, he had no intention of making a play for her. For several nights now he'd enjoyed the spice of knowing there was some powerful chemistry between them, and for a while there, when they were waltzing, he'd imagined . . . but no.

He was good at reading people's expressions, and he could tell from hers after the last dance that it wouldn't work out between them. She disapproved of how he made his living and mistrusted his pursuit of Neal. Perhaps she suspected him of being uncivilized. True, he hadn't spent much time in elegant social situations, and if it hadn't been for his mother, he wouldn't even know how to waltz.

How his mother had loved to dance. During breaks from her duties as cook for the ranch where they'd lived, she'd taken a battery-operated tape player out under a mesquite tree and conducted dance class for both him and Celia. She'd taught them the fox-trot, too, which he'd been able to translate easily in later years to the two-step. But the waltz had been her passion, and she'd schooled him mercilessly until his gangly fifteen-year-old body had obeyed the lush rhythm of the dance.

"If you want to know a woman, and let her know you, waltz with her," his mother had said.

And so he had waltzed with Dallas, and for the space of that song had believed he'd finally found a woman to fill his soul. But later, when the waltz no longer claimed her, her eyes had told him a different story. So he would check her trailer tonight and continue to watch over her. He would try to protect her from Neal Parnell and thereby attempt to avenge his little sister. But he would keep his hands off Dallas Wade from now on. Apparently she thought he wasn't good enough for her. He wouldn't try to convince her otherwise.

DALLAS HELPED AMBER restore order in the shop before heading for a bank of pay phones near the rest rooms to make her calls in private.

When Dallas returned, Amber confronted her, hands on hips. "What's going on? I've been dying of curiosity. I saw you two head for the dance floor. Did you ask him to help you?"

Dallas nodded. "He's coming out to check the security on my trailer," Dallas said, wiping the shampoo bowl with a damp towel. "I just called the two references he gave me and they think he's the greatest."

"I'm not surprised. When is he going to check the trailer?"

Dallas concentrated on the shine of the porcelain beneath her polishing towel. "Tonight. After we close up here."

"Wow. He works fast."

Dallas glanced up and caught Amber's grin. "Hey. He's only checking my locks."

"Wonder if I could get him to check mine."

"It's not what you think, Amber. He's sure Neal's about to try something."

"That may be. It's also a wonderful excuse to go home with you tonight. And I'll bet you're twisted in knots over the idea of being in close confines with that gorgeous cowboy."

Dallas returned to her polishing. "I've told you, Amber. I'm not interested in his type."

"Sure you're not. That's why you have that towel in a death grip. Look, your knuckles are white."

Dallas glanced down at the towel and tossed it into the dirty-clothes bin. "Nothing will happen," she said, more to herself than Amber.

"That's your loss, then," Amber said with another grin.

ON THE WAY HOME, with the lights of Gabe's old truck shining in her rearview mirror, Dallas struggled with the protocol of this visit. Should she offer him coffee? He was, after all, doing her a favor. But a cup of coffee might suggest more than she was prepared to handle. Better just let him check the locks and go home. Although she'd never feared living alone, she'd installed good locks because it seemed stupid not to, and the ones that had come with the trailer hadn't been adequate.

She pulled up in front of the chain-link fence, her headlights picking out Gretchen's fawn-colored coat as the dog barked a greeting.

Gabe parked beside her and swung down from his truck. He wore a faded denim jacket over his flannel shirt, making him look more like a rogue than ever. "I'm glad you have a dog," he said when she got out of her truck and walked toward him.

"I'm not sure if Gretchen would guard me or not." Dallas unlatched the gate and grabbed Gretchen's collar. "She's still young, and if you brought a male dog around to entice her, she'd be gone in a flash."

Gabe stepped through the gate and reached to scratch the dog's ears. "So it's like that, is it, Gretchen?"

"Down the road there's a huge dog, part Irish wolfhound and part Saint Bernard, who has designs on her." Dallas suspected she was babbling, but Gabe's presence beside her as they went up the walk was unnerving. "I've had to reinforce the fence to keep him out."

"And her in?" Gabe asked, a smile in his voice.

"Yes," Dallas admitted, unlocking the dead bolt. "If I left things up to her, she'd run off with the first mongrel that came along."

"But you have other plans for her." There was an edge to his voice as he walked into her pine-paneled living room, Gretchen close at his heels. He turned to face her. "Don't you?"

Dallas closed the door. "Yes. I'm not going to breed her now, and possibly not until she's about two years old. When I decide the time is right, I'll pick out a pedigreed stud."

He nodded and continued to scratch behind the dog's ears. "Can't have indiscriminate breeding. No telling what that could lead to."

"I have a feeling you don't approve of my plans for Gretchen." She took off her hat and ran her fingers through her hair. "Are you one of those people who thinks we should let nature take its course?"

He studied her for a moment without answering and her words seemed to echo between them. Her fingers trembled as she combed them back through her hair again.

Finally he shrugged. "I've met my share of pedigreed studs, and I've found the temperament of mongrels to be a whole lot better."

"Is that right?" Leaving her jacket on, she turned to hang her hat on the rack beside the door, as much to break contact with his compelling gaze as to be tidy. She had a feeling they weren't talking about dogs any longer. "Is that part of your problem with Neal?"

His jaw tightened. "It could be, but it isn't." He glanced around. "Do you have a back door to this place?"

"Near my bedroom. I'll show you."

She was aware of his tread behind her down the narrow hallway, could feel his gaze on her back, even the heat of his body in the small space. He was too close. If he touched her with those wonderful hands, would she be able to shrug away with the proper indignation? Or would she lean into his touch with a sigh and turn a waiting mouth up to his? She didn't want to test herself.

She walked past the door to give him access to it. She'd left a soft light on in her bedroom, as she always did, to welcome herself home. The white chenille spread was tucked neatly under the pillows, and pictures of her family were arranged artfully on her bedside table. She'd decorated with southwestern prints of Indian women against a backdrop of red cliffs and rustic pueblos.

His glance moved past her to the bedroom. "You have good taste."

"Thank you."

"Is there a gun in one of those bedside table drawers?"

She was startled. Most people didn't guess that there was. She nodded. "A Lady Smith & Wesson. Five shots."

"I know how many bullets it takes. Do you know how to use it?"

She faced him. "I grew up in west Texas. My daddy wasn't much of a family man, but he taught us all how to ride and shoot, how to mend a fence and put up a corral. You're not talking to a hothouse flower, Mr. Escalante."

"I didn't expect I was," he said, and turned to the door.

"I put in the locks."

He nodded and opened the door and a draft of cool air came in, making her realize how heated her skin had become.

She watched the movement of his fingers as he shot the bolt and tested it for strength. Tension built low in her pelvis. Could she manage a quick affair and be done with this craving? She knew the answer even before the question was fully formed. She'd never been the type; her passions ran deep. But they must not run with this man, no matter how he stirred her.

She tried to ignore the flex of his shoulder muscles as he pushed against the door. "He could always force these doors. He works out in a gym and I think he's in pretty good shape."

She had to concentrate to remember who Gabe was talking about. With Gabe around, she didn't have room in her mind for Neal. Gabe's scent surrounded her, pulling her in. "Would you like some coffee?" she blurted, desperate for an excuse to get away from him.

He turned, transfixing her with his deep-set eyes. "The usual answer is, 'If it's made,' but of course you don't have coffee ready."

"I'll make some." Why was she even offering? She didn't want him to linger and tempt her further.

"Don't bother. I'll be finished soon." He walked into the bedroom. "Let me check out these windows. It would suit him to come through one of them and surprise you before you're fully awake."

She balanced unsteadily against the wall as he put one knee on her bedspread and leaned toward the window over her bed. His jeans pulled tight across his buttocks, and she closed her eyes momentarily. Her hands were clammy. "I'm making coffee," she announced, and fled to the kitchen.

6

COWARD, DALLAS THOUGHT as she spooned coffee into the basket, scattering some over her clean counter in her haste. *He's only a man.* Her hand was steadier as she poured water into the coffeemaker and switched it on. She took off her jacket and hung it over a chair while listening to Gabe moving through her trailer locking and unlocking windows. Gretchen kept him company, judging by the accompanying jingle of dog tags.

By the time Gabe appeared in the kitchen she'd composed herself and could face him with a semblance of equanimity. "What's the verdict?"

A corner of his mouth tilted up. "You're a good carpenter."

The words of praise filled her with a ridiculous amount of pride. She cared too much about his opinion, she told herself sternly. "So you think I'm pretty well barricaded in?"

"Probably. Do you still have my card?"

She nodded.

"I have a machine and I check it regularly when I'm out. But call 911 first if Neal shows up. Gretchen will tell you if anyone's around." At the sound of her name Gretchen shoved her muzzle into his hand. "She might not attack," he continued, stroking the dog, "but you never know. You haven't had a chance to test her."

"True."

He rubbed Gretchen's head and her tail whapped back and forth, knocking against the kitchen door-frame. Dallas liked his manner with her dog. Most people kept their distance from Gretchen because of her size, but Gabe treated her with the nonchalance of someone used to big animals.

"Do you have a dog?" she asked.

"Can't. Wouldn't be fair with the kind of life I live." He squatted down so his face was level with Gretchen's and she responded by licking his cheek and knocking off his hat. Laughing, he picked it up and scrubbed a hand over her neck. "But I'd love to. I'd love to have a dog just like you, you big, clumsy, beautiful mutt."

Gretchen swiped her tongue over his face again.

"Wet kisses will get you anywhere," he said, laughing again.

Dallas stared at them as her image of Gabe tumbled into a new dimension. The sound of his laughter had surprised and charmed her. She'd become so used to his intensity she'd discounted the possibility of a softer side.

He glanced up at her. "I think the coffee's done."

With a start she turned to discover the coffeemaker had stopped gurgling.

"Smells good," he said, rising and setting his hat on the counter. "Guess I could use a cup, after all."

"Me, too." *Or something stronger.* She opened a cupboard and considered her collection of mugs. Each was different. Some had clever sayings inscribed on them; others she'd chosen for their beauty or connec-tion to a place she'd loved. Smack in the front of the shelf was the mug Amber had given her for Christmas. Hair Stylists Get You Lathered Up. Gabe was standing directly behind her. Unless his eyesight was bad, he could read the inscription easily. Damn. She didn't need more reminders of sex around here.

She reached for a mug she'd picked up at the Grand Canyon and another with a picture of a fawn-colored Great Dane on it. Then she closed the cupboard and poured the coffee. "Do you take anything in it?"

"No."

She schooled her expression to casual disinterest before turning to hand him the mug. He accepted it without comment.

"Your . . . your haircut isn't too bad."

"Thanks." He leaned one hip against the counter and Gretchen heaved herself down in front of him, nearly lying across his feet.

"Did you finish the job yourself?"

He shook his head and sipped his coffee.

For the first time it occurred to her he might have a girlfriend. She'd been arrogantly assuming she'd have to protect herself from his advances. Maybe he had no interest in her whatsoever, except as a damsel in distress. The thought chastened her.

"I wouldn't have pegged you as a Texas girl," he said, cradling the mug in both hands. "What happened to your accent?"

She sipped her coffee and wondered how much to reveal about herself. Every bit of information seemed to strengthen the link between them, and she shouldn't be doing that. "I took elocution lessons," she said at last.

He raised both eyebrows.

"I've always wanted my own business, and I decided a long time ago I'd have more success with banks and leasing companies if I dropped 'y'all' and 'honey' from my vocabulary." She neglected to mention that she didn't want to sound anything like her mother, who represented the worst side of feminine frailty to Dallas.

He seemed to accept her explanation. "You really think things through, don't you?"

"I've seen what happens when you don't." The declaration sounded prim and possibly judgmental, but she couldn't call it back.

Gabe chuckled and gazed at the ceiling. "Ah, yes."

"I guess we're not alike in how we look at things." First prim and now defensive. Where was her usual poise?

He pierced her with that warrior's stare. "No, we're not alike, Dallas."

She shouldn't like the way her name sounded when he said it. She shouldn't like the picture he made lounging in her kitchen in his worn jeans, his jacket open and the top two buttons of his shirt undone. By his subtle admission he was the sort of guy who took life as it came. Maybe she was a conservative prude, but now wasn't the time to fall for someone like Gabe. When he finished his coffee she'd send him on his way. Better not to learn more about this cowboy.

Then she remembered what Gabe had said to Neal at Rowdy Ranch. "I guess Neal thinks you're my boyfriend."

Gabe shrugged, his face expressionless. "At the time it seemed like the best way to make an impression on him." A ghost of a smile flickered. "If the idea bothers you I can tell him we broke up."

"Boy, that was quick." The retort masked a slight wrenching of her heart as he discussed their phantom relationship so casually. "Dumping me already."

"Your call," he said evenly. "I—"

Gretchen whined and leaped to her feet.

In one fluid movement Gabe set down his coffee and turned toward the living room door in a semicrouch as Gretchen stood in front of it, her ears pricked forward.

"Gabe, it could be—"

"Stay there." He crept toward the window and eased back the vertical blinds.

Dallas watched him in awe as adrenaline pumped through her. Gabe obviously was good at his job. The intruder could be Neal . . . or the mongrel down the street. Despite Dallas's brave words about the gun in her bedside table drawer and her confidence in her locks, she was trembling. And very glad to have someone like Gabe around right now.

"Dallas?"

"Yes?" She held her breath.

"Does Gretchen's boyfriend have long shaggy hair?"

She sighed with relief. "Yes." She walked to the door and took Gretchen by the collar. The tension, followed by a reprieve, made her giddy. "Not tonight, my eager young virgin."

Gretchen wouldn't budge from the door. She whined again and strained forward, as if she would hurl herself through the wooden barrier if Dallas gave her a chance.

Gabe let the vertical blind fall back into place and came over to kneel beside the dog and scratch behind her ear. "Hey, Gretch, he's an ugly son of a gun. You'd have really scruffy children."

Basking in the comradery of danger faced and unmasked, Dallas dropped to one knee on the dog's other side and threw an arm around Gretchen's neck. "Listen to the man. He doesn't like your choice any better than I do."

"I didn't say that."

Dallas's gaze snapped up to meet Gabe's. They eyed each other across Gretchen's head.

"I just said the puppies would be scruffy," he said gently. His fingers continued to massage behind Gretchen's ear, only inches away from where Dallas's arm lay draped around the dog's neck. "That doesn't mean they wouldn't be good dogs or that Gretchen and her friend wouldn't have a hell of a time making them."

An invisible fist squeezed her heart, then turned it loose to gallop in a furious rhythm. She swallowed. "Gretchen doesn't know what's good for her."

His dark gaze softened as his tone caressed her. "Maybe that mangy hound outside does."

Scraps of a waltz floated through her mind. She could feel his arms around her and his firm lead as they whirled around the floor. She'd never been loved by a man who didn't fumble. She put out a mental hand to steady herself. "Gabe, I—"

He reached over and placed a finger against her lips. She closed her eyes as he traced the outline of her mouth while he spoke. "I'm leaving now," he murmured. "Much as I don't want to. I don't even think you want me to."

Her mouth tingled; her body ached. No, she didn't want him to. "I have no more sense than Gretchen."

"Yes, you do." He cupped her chin and she opened her eyes. "You know exactly where you're going and what you want. I won't mess up your life for you, Dallas Wade." In one easy movement he rose and walked toward the kitchen to retrieve his hat. Pulling it low over his eyes, he opened the door. "Lock up after me."

GABE TOOK the trailer steps in one bound and headed out toward his truck. Another minute in that room with Dallas and he might have forgotten all his reservations about becoming involved with her. The huge mongrel slipped into the shadows as he opened the gate and walked to his truck.

"Better beat it," he said to the hulking canine. "Neither of us belongs inside that fence, amigo, no matter how much they flirt with us. We wouldn't be thanked for giving them what they want. You can count on it."

But restraint hadn't been easy, he thought, swinging up into the truck seat. He'd had a tough time ignoring the outline of her nipples through her soft cotton shirt, or her smooth thighs beneath shorts that mesmerized him with the dancing movement of the fringed hem. His groin tightened at the memory of Dallas turning to reach into the cupboard for coffee mugs. Hair Stylists Get You Lathered Up. No kidding.

As he maneuvered down the dirt lane toward the paved stretch of Avra Valley Road he almost missed the car parked beneath a mesquite. He glanced in the rear-view mirror to make sure the low-slung vehicle was a Corvette.

His pulse quickened and he relished the renewed challenge as just the distraction he needed right now. So the bastard was out there. Good. He'd tip his hand any time. And when he did, he was dead meat.

Gabe continued at the same pace, not letting on he'd noticed anything. The black car was deep in the shadows, and most people would have missed it. Gabe wondered when Parnell had decided to drive a black car. During the day it stood out, as he probably hoped it would. But after sunset the car was camouflaged by darkness and became nearly as invisible as other creatures of the night.

Gabe rolled down his window a fraction. Cold air wafted past his face as he listened for the sound of a car engine. He'd have to go back to Dallas's trailer, but he didn't want to let Parnell know about it. And he didn't want to take too long.

FOR SEVERAL MINUTES after Gabe left, Dallas leaned her forehead against the locked door and battled her emotions. She'd wanted him to kiss her. More than kiss her. And he hadn't done it. Why not?

Her image of him shifted yet again. She'd thought of him as aggressively sexual, someone she'd have to control. He'd controlled himself, and she didn't think it had anything to do with being faithful to another woman. Most men would have seized the opportunity to seduce a willing partner. Gabe hadn't done that. Obviously she'd underestimated him.

And now that he'd gone, what was she to do about the ache he'd left behind? Dallas wasn't used to men rejecting her for her own good. She didn't much like it. Gabe had been absolutely right to leave, and she was furious with him for having the strength to do it.

With a sigh she rolled around to lean her back against the door. "Guess we'd better hit the hay, Gretchen," she said, unbuttoning her blouse. "Neither of us is getting any action tonight."

A soft tap on the door brought her heart into her throat. She clutched Gretchen's collar and thought of the gun resting uselessly in the drawer a long, long way from where she stood.

"Dallas? It's Gabe."

Air whooshed out of her as she whirled toward the door. "Gabe?"

"Let me in. Now."

She hurried to obey and he slipped inside the door, bringing a cool wash of air with him.

He snapped the lock in place behind him and turned toward her. "Parnell's parked down the road."

Her hand went to her mouth. He was out there, after all. Breathing became more difficult as she fought feelings of panic.

"I circled back around and came in the other way. My truck's behind some creosote. I figured if he has plans, better if he tries something without knowing I'm still around. That way we have the element of surprise."

She stared at him. "You came through the wash? That's a terrible road."

"Yeah, it is," he said with a grin. "I may have lost a muffler on the trip."

"You look like—you look like you're *enjoying* yourself!"

He stuck his hands in the back pockets of his jeans and surveyed her from head to toe. "Some," he said, almost drawling the word, "although not nearly as much as I'd like. I'm trying to be a gentleman, Dallas, but you do make that a difficult proposition."

She glanced down at her unbuttoned blouse and flushed. "I was going to bed." She hastily refastened the buttons.

His voice rumbled low in his chest. "Let's not make any hasty invitations, lady."

"I wasn't! I—"

His laughter stopped her. "Relax, Dallas. I'm here to guard you from Parnell. That's all. If you have an extra pillow and blanket, I'll park on your denim sofa for the night, or until he shows himself."

"You think he really might?"

"I think it's only a matter of time before he tries something. Obviously you're still not convinced. I guess I understand that. Because if Parnell tries to rape you, you'll have to conclude he's probably raped before."

She lifted her chin. "That was a fair trial."

"Fairness isn't always justice. I prefer justice myself. But we could argue that point all night. Entertaining as that might be, I think you'd better get me that pillow and blanket."

Staying in her trailer all night? Dallas tried to imagine how that would work, with her hormones raging every time she looked at this tall cowboy. "Gabe, this seems like too much of a sacrifice on your part. Maybe we should call the sheriff."

"We could do that, but once a squad car enters the area Parnell will be gone. After that, we won't know where he is, and all the sheriff's department can offer is an occasional drive-by to check on you. I'd rather know where a rattlesnake is than scare him off and wonder where he'll turn up next."

She combed her hair back from her face. "You have a point." She glanced behind him to the sofa. "But you're not going to fit very well on that."

"Aw, shucks, Miss Dallas. Let's not get into a discussion of where I'll fit, thank you kindly."

She gazed up at him, her heart hammering in her chest. Why not just take him into her bed and be done with it?

"No," he said softly.

Again! He'd rejected her again. Without a word she whirled and stalked back to the linen closet. Could he interpret her thoughts so accurately? Apparently so. Maybe guessing what people were thinking was part of being a good bounty hunter. *It was part of being a good lover, too.* She'd never known a man who could read her so well. He'd be able to anticipate her needs, fulfill . . . dammit! She wrenched the pillow and blanket from the closet and stormed back with them.

"Here," she said, thrusting them forward.

"Such graciousness."

"You're confusing me." Now she sounded petulant. Terrific.

"Confusing you is preferable to a few other things I could be doing to you." He turned and tossed the pillow on the end of the sofa. "Good night, Dallas."

Dismissed, she left the room and walked back down the hall, her poise in riotous disarray. She wanted him so much she could taste it. And she didn't want him. But neither made any difference, because he was turning down the possibility. She closed her bedroom door with a little more force than necessary.

"Don't lock it," he called out. "You might need me during the night."

She just knew he'd said that on purpose.

7

GRETCHEN'S SHORT BARK woke Dallas. Disoriented in the darkness, she propped herself on one elbow. "What is it, girl?" she mumbled.

Gretchen barked again, then growled and faced the window over Dallas's bed. With a cry Dallas bolted from the bed and wrenched open her door. On the other side she collided with Gabe, who was still buttoning his jeans.

He moved quickly around her to the dog. "Is he out there, Gretchen?" he asked softly.

"She b-barked at the window." Dallas wrapped her arms around her body to try to stop the shaking. The luminous clock dial on her bedside table read three-thirty.

Gabe walked quietly to the drawer beneath it and took out Dallas's handgun. Checking the chambers in the light from the clock face, he came back and offered it to her, butt first. "I'm going out the back door to take a look. Lock it after me."

"You should take the gun."

"I work better without one. Always have."

Dallas wondered if she'd be able to hit the broad side of a barn the way she was shaking, but not a tremor passed over Gabe as he slipped to the door, opened it and stepped into the night. She opened her mouth to call him back, but he was gone before the words came out.

Locking the door as he'd ordered, she padded into the living room to wait in the dark. She could dimly make out the blanket and pillow he'd tossed on the floor in his haste to get up. He must have come instantly awake to pull on boots and jeans in that short time from Gretchen's first bark to the moment she'd collided with him in the hall.

It took two tries before she managed to pick up the blanket in her nerveless fingers. She wrapped it around her shoulders before sitting in the rocker, the gun resting on her knee. She'd bought the gun, practiced with it, bragged to Gabe about knowing how to use it, but she'd never really expected to. She even hated to shoot rattlesnakes and usually called the fire department to transport them farther out into the desert. If she couldn't shoot a snake, how could she be expected to take aim at a man? Some tough broad she was.

She rocked nervously back and forth while Gretchen paced the room, whining. The blanket held Gabe's scent, and Dallas brought it to her nose and inhaled. Gabe, out there facing unknown danger in the cold darkness, had stayed the night to protect her. Her stomach hollowed with dread. He was trained for this, she reminded herself. He knew how to hunt men, how to outwit them. He would be okay. The need to have him safe again grew steadily as she waited.

Gretchen whined again.

"Be quiet, Gretch," she whispered, trying to hear any noises from outside. A pack of coyotes yipped in the distance, and an owl hooted from somewhere nearby, but Dallas heard nothing that sounded like a scuffle. What if Neal had been lying in wait and had already knocked Gabe unconscious? What if he was prying open a window in the bathroom, where she might not hear him? She wrapped the comforting blanket tighter and pretended Gabe was holding her.

Besides, Gretchen would alert her to someone coming in. The dog kept up her interminable pacing.

At last someone tapped on the back door. Her heart pounding, she dropped the encumbering blanket and started cautiously toward the door, gun cocked.

"It's me," Gabe said from the other side of the door.

The sound of his voice sent her chilled blood singing through her veins again. She let him in, along with a gust of frigid early-morning air. "What happened?"

He relocked the door. Blowing on his hands and rubbing them together, he turned to her. "Couldn't find a thing, but I'll bet anything he was out there, saw me come out the back door and took off. Bullies don't enjoy being evenly matched. He thought I was gone and you were fair game. I doubt he'll be back tonight." He glanced down. "Would you mind pointing that somewhere else?"

"Oh!" She lowered the gun, which she'd been holding waist high, aimed right at him.

"God knows I've done a few things I deserve to be shot for, but I'd as soon not go out that way, if you don't mind."

Feeling like a fool, Dallas eased the hammer back in place and started toward the bedroom. "I'll put it away. Sounds like the danger's over for the night."

Behind her, he let out a shaky sigh. "I wish I could say that."

She turned in surprise. "But I thought you said—"

"Put the gun away. Parnell won't be back."

"Then what—"

"For a smart lady, you can be damned stupid."

He stood unmoving, a dark shadow just outside her bedroom door. In the weighted silence she remembered that she wore only her nightgown, a white-lace-and-chiffon affair that reached to mid-thigh. He might not be able to see her well, but obviously he could see her well enough. And imagination could be more powerful than sight.

Slowly she rested the gun on the dresser beside her. A word from her and he'd return to his bed on the sofa. He'd proven his iron will, but now she could hear his rapid breathing and knew that his will was being tested. She trembled but stood her ground, her body tightening in response to his quiet presence.

His voice sounded strained. "Come and close this door."

"No," she whispered.

With a soft oath he stepped over the threshold and kicked the door shut. "I promised myself I wouldn't do this."

"So did I."

He crossed the room. "Then we're both fools." With a groan of surrender he reached for her.

She fit perfectly in his arms, as she had on the dance floor. Except now she enjoyed the entire length of his rock-solid body, and her own seemed to swell with promise in response to the coiled power of his. She ran both hands up his back and felt his muscles contract beneath her touch.

His large callused hand cupped her cheek in the darkness and she closed her eyes to savor the controlled passion in his caress. He seemed in no hurry to kiss her, as if he wanted their bodies to shimmer with heat until they burst into flame with the first touch of their mouths. When his fingers brushed across her parted lips, she wet his fingertips with her tongue and his breath caught.

He combed her hair back from her face and cradled her head as he leaned close enough for her to feel his soft breath on her face. "A cowboy's dream," he murmured, closing the distance until she was submerged in his embrace, dazed by the unleashed power of his kiss.

His mouth claimed her with a sureness that left her no time to think. She gasped, helpless before the onslaught of emotions he drew forth. She was not the sort of woman to whimper, but she whimpered now. He stroked the length of her body and brought her hard against him. Her first quivering response turned to molten desire beneath the force of his compelling touch.

Her thighs were slick with moisture even before his knowing hand slid between their bodies to find her. He made a noise deep in his throat, a sound of appreciation so basic it sent goose bumps skittering over her skin. He urged her against the bed. When the backs of her knees touched the mattress, he lowered her down across the edge of it, his mouth hard against hers.

He groped for the handle of the bedside table drawer and wrenched it open. Vaguely she realized he had to have known what the drawer contained as he unbuttoned his jeans and sheathed himself.

The ache within her widened, crying to be filled. He didn't bother to remove his shirt or her nightgown. With one hand braced beside her head and the other guiding her hips, he took her in one strong, deliberate thrust that made her gasp. Never had a man claimed her like that. Never had she quivered with the beginnings of a climax with only one sure stroke.

Ah, but never was over. Gabe was here. He eased back and shoved home once more. Her body welcomed him, throwing down all barriers and inviting him back again. And again. In wanton delight she lifted her hips and wrapped her legs around his waist, bringing him closer and deeper. Each time he came to her, ripples of pleasure spread from the pulsing center of their joining with an increasing intensity that left her breathless.

She began to spin on the axis of that center as she begged incoherently—whether for more sensation or final release she didn't know. Only he could know. His touch filled her universe, his body held every delight she'd ever imagined.

The flowering began slowly, then picked up speed as she unfolded in a dazzling display of surrender that wrung a cry of wonder from her lips. Annointed with passion, she clung to him as he answered her cry with one of his own, a sound that seemed to arise from deep within his soul. His massive body shuddered once, twice, a third time, and his fingers pressed against her skin.

Slowly, slowly his bunched muscles relaxed. While they were still joined he eased her forward until they could lie together. He remained braced above her, not giving her his full weight, as he leaned his damp forehead against hers.

She held him, rubbing her hands across his back as a measure of sanity returned. Perhaps she wouldn't ever be quite sane again where this man was concerned. He'd just given her the most satisfying sexual experience of her life. Did she have the inner strength to put that memory aside? Not tonight, she thought. Definitely not tonight.

He sighed and lifted his head to gaze at her in the dim light. "Ah, Dallas," he murmured, touching her cheek. "You don't inspire a man to be subtle."

She caught his hand and kissed his palm, savoring the taste of him, the scent of him. "And who says subtle is good?"

"You might."

He'd changed her world and he didn't even know it. She was touched by his modesty...and insecurity. "Did you follow your instincts?"

"Every single one of them."

"I'd say you have pretty good instincts."

She felt the quiver that ran through him, but he said nothing, as if waiting, his breath held, for her to go on. He deserved the truth, no matter where it led them. "I've never been loved so well, Gabe." She chose the word "loved" on purpose, because she'd never felt as valued as now, never as sensual or desirable.

His face relaxed into a smile. "Thank you for telling me that."

"I can't believe you didn't know."

His smile widened. "Women have been known to fake it."

"I don't."

"No, I don't suppose you do."

She ran her fingers up his nape and through the thick luxury of his hair, remembering when she'd first done that, when he was seated in her chair at work. Had she known, even then, that one day she'd hold him like this? "I have a question. How did you know I had condoms in the drawer?"

"After I checked your window lock in here I opened both drawers to find out which one had the gun in it. I suppose I've been thinking about that package of condoms ever since. It didn't make resisting you any easier, knowing they were there within easy reach."

"So you snooped!" She struggled and tried to roll out from under him, but he held her fast.

"I checked things out." He raised his head and dropped quick, conciliatory kisses on her lips as he spoke. "I'm a careful man, Dallas. That's what's allowed me to survive this long in a dangerous profession."

She shuddered, even as she found herself responding to the warm kisses raining on her mouth. "I don't like to think about that."

"I know. We don't have to. At least not now. Don't go away." He levered himself away from her, got up and went into the bathroom. Moments later he returned. Lying beside her, he began working on the tiny buttons of her nightgown that reached down to the middle of her breasts.

"Have you ever come close to being killed?" she asked.

"As I said, let's not think about that."

Her breath quickened as he parted the lapels of her gown and cupped her breast in his palm. "What should we think about, then?"

"This." He stroked her nipple with his thumb and the firmness of his renewed desire pressed against her thigh. As he leaned down to run the tip of his tongue around the areola of her throbbing breast, she could think of nothing but his moist caress.

Then he took her nipple in his mouth, building the tension that caused her to move her hips in restless invitation. In so many ways he was the wrong man for her, but at this moment, in this bed, nothing had ever felt so right.

GABE USED HIS TEETH to scrape lightly over her nipple, and she arched her back in the age-old gesture of submission to her man. His heartbeat pounded loud in his ears as that simple gesture stirred the hot embers of his need to take her again. The sharp edge of the first time had been replaced by a deepening ache that frightened him just a little. But not enough to stop.

He slid an arm under her shoulder blades to support the arch that offered her breasts to his questing mouth. She tasted of honey, smelled like crushed wildflowers fermenting into a heady wine. He burrowed against her with his seeking mouth. Ah . . . the texture of her nipple against the curved pull of his tongue, the bounty of her breast drawn into his mouth, brought pounding tension to his groin. Yet he'd already demonstrated impatience. Perhaps this time he had the strength to demonstrate restraint.

With a superhuman force of will he subdued his own desire to fill her and settled his mouth between her breasts. While continuing to tease her nipples to erectness with his fingertips, he kissed a path downward, stopping to dip his tongue into her navel. Her fingers dug into his shoulders as he continued his journey over the smooth skin of her belly and the soft tangle of hair between her thighs. When he reached his destination she trembled. He wanted to hear her cries, now, when he wasn't buried in her and deafened by the cannon fire of his own needs.

He nibbled and tasted the rare fruit of her passion, grasping her hips when he'd driven her beyond the ability to keep still. She moaned, and he probed more boldly, feeling her swell beneath him. Her first, small panting cries ignited a fierce happiness in him. He never remembered giving pleasure with this much joy. He kept on as her legs quivered and her cries grew stronger, until at last she bucked in his arms and gasped his name. His name. He was not some featureless lover.

Driven by a desire that left him no choice, he pulled the latex tight over his throbbing penis and claimed his due, sinking deep, deep into salvation. He felt her tighten again, and the spasms of her second climax drew the essence from him in one great rush. As he lay against her, dazed and panting, he knew that she'd seared his heart, changed his direction. After this night, he would never be the same man again.

"EVER BEEN MARRIED, Gabe?" Dallas stopped placing strips of bacon side by side on the microwave rack and turned to where he was frying eggs in a skillet on the stove. She'd let Gretchen out to run in the yard, so they were alone. Early-morning light gave the kitchen a soft-focus look, which suited her blissful mood after the dazzling amount of pleasure she'd enjoyed the night before.

"Yes, I've been married." He glanced up with those impenetrable eyes of his. "Why?"

"Why?" She shook her head. "Only a man would ask why a woman wants to know that. Don't you understand that it matters a lot?"

"To who? Or is it 'whom'?"

"Now *that* doesn't matter, but the fact of your marriage matters to anyone you—" She paused. Maybe she'd just backed herself into a corner. They'd spent the night together, shared the chore of feeding the horses this morning and decided on bacon and eggs for breakfast, but that's as far into their combined future as they'd ventured. "Well, it's important to anyone who wants to know more about you."

His mouth quirked. "I assume that includes you."

She nodded and went back to her bacon, pretending great interest in aligning the slices on the rack. "So, once or more than once?"

"Once."

She cast him a covert glance and discovered his attention was on the skillet in front of him.

He eased the spatula under an egg and flipped it over. "That bacon going to be done soon?"

"Yes." She shoved the bacon in the microwave and set the timer. "Will you tell me about your marriage?"

"Not much to tell."

Dallas raised her eyes heavenward. If only some men had little buttons in their necks marked "communication mode." Obviously it wasn't this man's normal setting, but he definitely needed an override button for certain situations, and this was one. "You could start with a few facts, like when you got married, how long you stayed married, if you had any children, if you see them, if you see her, if she's pretty." That last was actually more important to Dallas than some of the other things she'd mentioned. But you couldn't trust a man's evaluation of pretty, either. Still, she'd like to know his opinion of his former wife. Was she living in Tucson? Did she repair bad haircuts?

Gabe flipped another egg. He'd obviously spent many years cooking for himself. "Eggs are ready."

The microwave dinged and with a sigh Dallas took out the bacon. When they'd filled their plates and poured the coffee, they sat across from each other at her small oak table. She really had no right to pester him about his past loves, she thought, as she peppered her eggs. They'd spent one night together, and even she had no idea where they were going from here. The question had popped out, and she'd better pay attention to what that said about her motives, conscious or unconscious. The more she thought about it, the more she wanted to call her question back.

"Forget what I asked you a while ago," she said. "It's none of my business."

"Are you going to be able to find your eggs under all that pepper?"

She stared down at her plate in dismay. Her eggs looked as if they'd been directly under Mount Saint Helens when it erupted.

He reached over and took the pepper shaker out of her hand, keeping hold of her hand in the process. "It is your business," he said gently. "I'm not used to talking about my personal life, that's all."

"I understand." She tried to pull her hand away. "I was prying. I didn't mean to."

His voice was soft. "Didn't you?"

"Okay. I want to know about you, Gabe."

His thumb brushed her knuckles. "You were right last night. We are different. But in some ways we're not. Neither of us is halterbroke." His smile was wry. "That's why my marriage didn't work out."

She stiffened. "I have no intention of tying you down."

"I know." He continued to caress her hand. "But like it or not, sometime during the night we passed the point of no return. No matter what happens now, we'll always be important to each other. We can't change that. Not now."

8

DALLAS LOOKED at their clasped hands, his blunt and workmanlike, hers tapered and pale in contrast. The point of no return. She hadn't thought it through, but she understood what he meant. Her inner debate over whether to consider a relationship with Gabe was over. In a night filled with intimate moans and whispered desires, a relationship had begun.

"The way I see it," he began, "you could use someone around for a few days, until something happens with Parnell."

She glanced into his eyes with a half smile. "How about for a few nights?"

"That, too."

A thrill ran through her at the look in his eyes. He'd unmasked his desire, allowed her to see how much he wanted her. He was far from revealing all his thoughts to her, but he no longer bothered to keep his passion a secret. He'd told her during the night how she'd affected him with her sensuous washing of his hair, how he'd tamped down his reaction to her from that moment on. From the expression on his face now, he was tamped down no longer.

"It's been a long time since I've had a roommate," she confessed. "I'm not sure how good I am at sharing my space."

"I'm not sure I'm any good at it, either. You might as well know I've been accused of being moody and stubborn."

She laughed. "No, really?"

"Yeah." He grinned and released her hand. "Our breakfast's getting cold. I'll tell you all about my failed marriage to Anna while we eat, if it won't ruin your appetite."

Anna. He'd said her name with a certain tenderness that unleashed jealousy in Dallas, an emotion she probably had no reason for or right to. She'd spent one night with this man, and she had no claims. Yet her attempt to listen dispassionately failed, and she barely tasted her food as Gabe talked of his former love.

Gradually a story emerged of two people who had married young and struggled with financial problems. He discussed Anna's inability to conceive, which bothered her more than it did him. Gabe's portrait of his ex-wife was compassionate, but Dallas could tell he thought of Anna as a child who had expected him to direct her every move. Dallas took comfort in knowing she and Anna were very different.

"Then I got into the bail-enforcement business. Turned out I liked it a lot, and she hated everything about it—the potential for violence, the uncertain hours, the trips out of the country."

Dallas listened carefully. Was he giving her a warning about the helter-skelter life he lived?

"Anna discovered she couldn't live for weeks at a time without someone helping her make decisions. She turned to Jose, who helped her decide to divorce me and marry him, instead." His words sounded matter-of-fact, but a catch in his voice told Dallas the hurt and sense of betrayal still lingered.

"Did you ever consider giving up—" Dallas paused and was careful to choose the right term "—bail enforcement?"

"No. I used to think I was a quiet, family-man type, but I've discovered I'm not. Maybe, if we'd had kids, I might have become like that."

Dallas studied Gabe over the rim of her coffee mug and tried to imagine him as a domesticated male. "I doubt it."

"Yeah," he admitted with a sigh. "Me, too. You know that song about a little less talk and a lot more action? I'm a real fan of that song." He pushed back his chair. "And right now I've had about all the sitting around I can take for a while. What are your plans for the day?"

Dallas had been so engrossed in thinking about Gabe in action, a concept she cherished despite her misgivings about his profession, that she had to stop and think. Of course she had plans for the day. Her free time was crammed with projects and the work never seemed to get done. But having Gabe here had drummed everything right out of her mind. "It's Saturday, right?" she said, feeling foolish for having to ask.

"Unless last night changed the moon and stars, I do believe it's Saturday. But anything's possible."

"I'll take that as a compliment."

His gaze softened. "Be my guest."

She hesitated, wanting to say this right. "I . . . appreciate your confiding in me."

"No problem."

She knew he wasn't as offhand about their discussion as he'd like her to believe, but at least he'd allowed her a look behind his forbidding exterior. Not long ago he'd been punished for being himself. That explained a lot about his wariness. Not that he'd been transformed into an open book. The air of mystery surrounding him remained, even when he smiled. Sometimes especially when he smiled.

"If it's Saturday," she said, "I'm scheduled to pick up four bales of hay, muck out the corral, reset a fence post, give Gretchen a bath and hot-oil treatment, do a load of wash and call my mother."

He leaned back on two legs of the chair. "That's all? And here I thought you might be busy."

"How about you? What's on your agenda?"

"Keeping you safe."

Her smile faded as she remembered the terror she'd experienced the night before. Being in Gabe's arms until dawn had temporarily blotted out that frightening moment when Gretchen's bark had announced an intruder. Or had it really been an intruder? In the daylight Dallas was inclined to believe the disturbance could as easily have been a neighbor's cat as Neal Parnell.

She stood and began clearing the breakfast dishes. "Maybe we're overreacting here."

There was a sudden stillness about him, like an animal pausing to test the air. Then he picked up the remaining dishes and followed her to the sink. "Meaning?"

She shrugged. "I appreciate the thought, but I hardly think my safety constitutes a twenty-four-hour job. I'm sure you have some things to do. I feel as if this is keeping you from your work."

"My work is sporadic," he said, almost too casually. "But I don't want to crowd you. Your safety can also be guaranteed if I follow Parnell, so if you'd like me to make myself scarce, I can oblige."

She turned. The cautious look on his face told her the ease they'd achieved with each other was balanced precariously on this topic, but she had trouble sharing his obsession about Parnell. After all, the guy hadn't really *done* anything yet. Maybe he would still fade away, and she wouldn't have to worry about him or his implied threat to her financial security. She hesitated to tell Gabe what Neal had said about knowing her banker. Gabe would only get even more riled up about the guy.

But all that aside, she longed to know Gabe better, and she reached to retrieve the closeness they'd found during breakfast. "I could use some help mucking out the corral, if you aren't allergic to a shovel," she said, keeping her tone light. "And if your back's up to loading the hay in my truck, I wouldn't turn down that offer, either."

He nodded, but his openness had disappeared. "Okay. I need to get some clothes, take care of some odds and ends, but I can be back in less than two hours, if you want to put those things off until then."

"Sure." She stuck her hands in the pockets of the jeans she'd put on after her morning shower. "Want to help with the dog, too?"

"I can do that."

She cursed silently to herself. He was like a desert tortoise—one loud noise and he pulled into that armored shell of his. She wished she could have known him without Neal being part of the picture, but, of course, she'd never have met Gabe without Neal. She wanted to probe into that whole business and find out what really drove Gabe to shadow Neal, but now was obviously not the time to get some answers.

He tipped his head toward her kitchen wall phone. "Can I make some calls?"

"Certainly." She hated the formality that caused him to have to ask. While she rinsed the dishes she tried not to listen in on the conversation, but it was tough not to hear because Gabe took no particular pains to keep his messages private.

He talked with someone named Diego and asked him to track down Parnell, who was probably sleeping off the night's activities at his apartment. Then he covered the mouthpiece and turned to her. "I need to give my friend the number here, if it's okay."

"It's okay." She wondered if they'd bridge this gap between them once again or if they'd discover they were totally incompatible, that the night before had been a fluke, and they were better off going their separate ways. She sighed and began stacking the dishes in the dishwasher.

He hung up the phone and walked toward her. "I'll be back about ten. Anything you need from town?"

She glanced up at him. "A half-gallon of coffee ice cream. I'll get you some mo—"

"Never mind that." He grabbed his jacket and started out the door. "Thanks for breakfast."

After the door closed Dallas smacked her hand down on the kitchen counter so hard her palm stung. But she was glad she'd asked for the ice cream. It looked as if she was going to need that ice cream.

ALL THE WAY BACK to his apartment, Gabe lectured himself for being twenty kinds of a fool. Sure, Dallas had enjoyed last night as much as he had, but she wasn't losing her head. She, at least, had the sense to put some distance between them. Not an impulsive person, that one. But he, on the other hand, seemed driven by his impulses.

The pattern was becoming depressingly familiar. Once again he'd allowed his emotions to rule where Dallas was concerned, and once again she'd brought him crashing back to reality. Now it was time to mop up.

Sparse Saturday-morning traffic didn't demand much of his attention, leaving him free to assess his situation with Dallas. The smart thing would be to stay out of her bed, but he knew himself better than that. With the experience of loving her so fresh, the excitement still humming through him, he couldn't walk away from the chance of holding her again. Maybe in a few days, when the novelty had worn off, he'd be able to walk away. Or maybe she'd walk away herself. Probably she would be the one. But she wasn't doing that now. For whatever her reasons, she wanted more or she wouldn't have invited him back to share her chores. He was at least smart enough to figure that out.

But was he smart enough to get through this brief affair unscathed? His best chance, he reasoned, was if he didn't allow her under his skin, didn't repeat this morning's idiocy of pouring out his heart to her. He'd explained why Anna had left him in terms that probably reminded Dallas why she didn't want a permanent relationship, either. She was a lot different from Anna, a lot more independent, but that didn't mean she'd be happy with a guy who lived the way he did.

What was it she'd said? *Maybe we're overreacting.* Once again, she wanted to downplay the threat of Parnell. He could have told her about Celia, probably should have. Except he could guess how she'd respond. She'd accuse him of lacking objectivity and using Parnell as a scapegoat. He couldn't tell her yet. He needed to wait until there was a chance she'd believe Parnell raped Celia. Right now she was still clinging to the verdict she'd helped deliver.

In the meantime, he needed to remember to pick up his six-pack cooler from his apartment. She'd asked for ice cream, and he'd be damned if he'd bring it to her melted.

DALLAS WAS PUTTING AWAY the last of her clean clothes when Amber called.

"So?" Amber said. "How did last night go?"

"Uh . . ." Dallas should have expected Amber to call and find out what Gabe had thought of her security system.

"Okay, my imagination is going wild, so you might as well tell me."

"He . . . thinks my locks are fine." Dallas felt herself blushing. How could she admit to Amber that she, who always lectured about caution in relationships, had thrown it to the winds last night?

"Dallas! Something happened between you two last night, didn't it?"

You could say that. "Well, after he left he saw Neal's car parked down the road and—"

"At two in the morning? I *told* you that guy was dangerous. Then what?"

"Um, Gabe came back and we decided, that is, it seemed the right thing to do at the time, for him to stay on the couch."

Amber was so quiet on the other end Dallas thought she might have been put on hold.

"Amber? You still there?"

"You little fox. You slept with him, didn't you?"

Dallas's shaky intake of breath was all the answer necessary.

"That good, was he?"

"Amber, I know you must think I'm out of my mind. He's definitely not my type. But I guess, with all that's happened, I got carried away."

Amber hooted with laughter. "Not your type? Lady, a hunk like that is *every* woman's type. I saw you guys dancing together last night, and I kind of wondered if the two of you would get together. But then I decided you were too uptight to let that happen. Guess I was wrong, huh?"

"Amber, I—" She paused as Gabe's battered truck pulled up outside the gate. "Listen, he's back. I'll have to go."

"What? Is he staying there with you now? Dallas, you can't just leave me hanging. Tell me what—"

Dallas watched Gabe come inside the gate, pet Gretchen and throw a ball she held in her mouth. Then he started toward the steps leading to her door. "Bye, Amber. And please don't make a big deal of this at work tonight, okay?"

"I can't even tell Dave?"

"Don't you *dare* tell Dave. Goodbye." Dallas hung up the phone just as Gabe tapped on the door.

Her heartbeat had quickened from the moment his truck appeared outside her gate. His soft rap on her door sounded like a rifle shot, making her jump even though she'd expected it. Her sweaty palm slipped on the doorknob and she had to wipe her hand on her jeans before she opened the door.

He stood on her front steps, his worn black cowboy hat shading his mysterious eyes, a gym bag held loosely in one hand and a small cooler in the other. "Coffee ice cream, right?"

She nodded as he held out the cooler. She took it and their fingers brushed, a little flick of awareness that traveled to all the sensitive spots on her body. "I always do that, bring it home in a cooler so it won't melt," she said.

"I figured you did." He held up his gym bag. "Where do you want me to put my stuff?"

"Oh, anywhere." She clutched the cooler with shaking fingers. He was back. Back to spend the day. To spend the night after work. To make love to her.

He met her gaze. The tilt of his hat gave him a renegade's glance that seemed almost insolent. "I don't want to clutter things up."

She swallowed as that glance brought a trembling lightness to her limbs. She didn't want to wait hours to feel his body entwined with hers. "You won't."

"I already have, haven't I?"

Tension pulsed between them. He'd been gone a mere two hours, and she felt as if she hadn't seen him in weeks. She wanted to touch him, be touched. "No," she murmured. "No, you haven't cluttered anything up."

He tossed the gym bag to the couch. The hat sailed after it. "Then maybe I should start."

She read his intent in his midnight eyes even before he took the cooler from her nerveless fingers and set it on the end table. When he reached for her she groaned.

"Was this on your agenda?" he asked, pulling her against him, letting her feel the hardening of his body.

She could only gaze up helplessly as his sculpted warrior's lips descended on hers. At first his mouth was hard and demanding, but as she returned the force of his kiss with equal frustration, he gentled, skimming his hands over her body as if to connect with every inch of her.

Breathing hard, he lifted his head. "I thought about this every mile of the way back. I told myself you had work to do."

"Damn the work." She fumbled with the buttons of his shirt and pushed her hands inside the soft flannel. His heart thumped against the palm of her hand as she pressed it against his chest. She looked up and saw his mask had slipped once again to reveal the passion she stirred in him. Maybe they couldn't talk without having him close himself off, but they could do this.

She scratched her fingernails lightly across the hair-sprinkled contours of his chest, and he drew in his breath. Reaching for her hand, he guided it down past the cold metal of his belt buckle to the straining denim over his erection. As she cupped him, he closed his eyes and shuddered.

Needing him in ways she'd never needed before, she unfastened the buckle and unbuttoned his fly as she gradually lowered herself to her knees.

He grasped her shoulders and started to pull her up. "Dallas, no, I—"

"Yes." She released him from the soft cotton of his briefs and stroked him with bold insolence. "Yes," she said again, before loving him with lips and tongue until he gasped and told her to stop. This time she obeyed and he swung her up in his arms.

In the bedroom they tore off his remaining clothes and hers. A step ahead of him, she took a condom from the drawer. When it was in place, he lay on his back on the bed and drew her on top of him. As she settled over his throbbing shaft his dark eyes burned into hers, almost as if he resented the sensual power she held over him. She reached down and smoothed the furrows from between his eyes. "So fierce," she whispered. "Give in, my warrior."

His jaw clenched. "I have."

"No." She began to move, circling her hips and rocking back and forth. "Not really."

He moaned and clutched her hips as she pleasured him. He threw his head back as she brought him closer to surrender. The tightening had begun for her, too, but she concentrated on Gabe, on releasing him from the demons that seemed to be driving him. "Let go," she whispered. "Let me take you away."

The tension grew in her; she closed her eyes against its force. A low sound came from deep in his chest and she opened her eyes to find him gazing at her, desire blazing forth as he thrust upward, deepening the contact.

And for that moment, pressed together just before the cataclysm claimed them both, she knew everything she needed to know about him. Then they tumbled together into the abyss.

9

THE MAN KNEW his way around a bale of hay, Dallas concluded after Gabe had unloaded her truck, stacked the hay and covered it with a tarp. They'd planned the chores carefully in order to accomplish everything in the shortened amount of time that remained after their lovemaking. They'd gone together to buy the hay, but he'd been assigned to unload it and dig the new fence post while she gave Gretchen her bath and hot-oil treatment.

Gabe had convinced Dallas not to shower until later, so she'd felt sinfully decadent moving through the day with Gabe's scent clinging to her, a subtle reminder of what they'd shared. Each time she glanced in his direction she wanted to stretch and purr like a well-fed cat. Concentrating on the chores that she'd assigned herself proved difficult, especially when Gabe took off his shirt before starting in on the posthole.

"Pretty sexy there, Escalante," she called over to him as she moved the hose over Gretchen's water-darkened coat.

He glanced up from the two-handled posthole digger and grinned, his teeth flashing white beneath the shadow of his hat. "Think I should charge extra for the floor show?"

"I doubt if I could afford it."

"For you, *señorita*, I make a special price," he said, and laughed before sinking the posthole digger into the soft earth. Sunlight reflected off the sheen of sweat on his muscled back as he worked.

Dallas bit her lip to keep from moaning out loud as he pounded the round metal into the ground again and again. This was ridiculous. She was worse than Gretchen panting after the hulking dog down the road. She'd never been at such a fever pitch that everything took on erotic overtones. She forced her gaze back to the dripping dog, who was beginning to shiver as the sun sank toward the mountain-rimmed horizon. "Sorry, girl," Dallas said, turning the nozzle and shutting off the stream of water. "I sure understand your problem a lot better now."

Later she and Gabe managed to shower without tumbling into bed only because Dallas wouldn't dream of stranding Amber with a big Saturday-night crowd. Dallas and Gabe planned to eat at the buffet provided by Rowdy Ranch, so they didn't have to worry about cooking.

"We can have ice cream when we get home, though," she said as they headed out to her truck for the trip to town. "I think it will be refrozen by then." The ice cream had been another casualty of their passion. By the time they'd remembered it, the carton had been soft and the contents soupy. "I'd also thought we could take a ride today," she said, casting a longing glance back at Sugar and Spice.

Gabe laughed as he opened the driver's door for her. "I think we did."

"Stop talking like that," she said, giving him a warning glance. "Or I won't be able to do my job tonight, just thinking about..." She left the sentence unfinished, suddenly shy.

"Say it," he murmured, glancing up at her, his hand caressing her thigh. "Thinking about my hands here, and here, and my mouth—"

"Gabe!" She pushed him away, but she was already steaming with fresh desire.

A smile on his face, he rounded the truck and climbed in beside her. "Don't forget, Parnell assumes I'm your lover. We wouldn't want him to think any different, would we?"

"With the way you affect me, nobody in the entire dance hall will think any different." She started the engine.

Gabe settled back in his seat, the same contented smile on his face. "Good."

THEY WALKED into Rowdy Ranch together, Gabe's arm slung casually around Dallas's shoulder. She felt like a star arriving at the Academy Awards as heads turned and eyes widened. None of the employees at Rowdy Ranch had ever seen her with a boyfriend. She hadn't dated much in the eighteen months she'd owned the shop, and she'd never brought one of her dates here.

"You're as tense as a roped calf," Gabe murmured as they walked toward the Cutting Pen.

"That's about how I feel. I'm not in the habit of parading my personal life in front of the world."

"Neither am I, toots. Gonna give me a kiss before you start work?"

"My God, Gabe."

"I spotted Parnell over by the pinball machines. He hasn't taken his eyes off us. Might as well make this roping look real."

They neared the pool tables, where Dave Fogarty stood, holding a pool cue and staring. Dallas couldn't look at him.

"Would you ordinarily kiss somebody in public?" she asked.

"That depends." He turned to face her and took off her red Stetson.

"Gabe, I—"

"You're beautiful, you know that?"

And before she could react he had pulled her into his arms. His kiss didn't take long, but he accomplished a lot in a short time. She was trembling from the passion he'd conveyed as he released her with a smile and set her hat back on her head, giving the brim a tug. "Have a good evening," he said softly. "And get rid of those damn roses." Then he headed toward the rack of pool cues.

Dallas struggled to reclaim her shattered composure as she walked into the shop where Amber stood transfixed, her manicure tray clutched against her chest. Dallas's greeting was a little too bright and shaky around the edges.

"Wow," Amber breathed. "What an entrance."

"It's . . . part of a plan." Dallas stowed her purse in a cabinet. Then she took the roses from the vase and dropped them in the trash.

Amber watched her with a knowing smile. "Some plan. Wish I could get Vince to make a plan like that."

"No, I mean, we're trying to fool Neal into think-ing—" she sounded out of breath and paused to take in air "—that we're serious about each other." Her face felt hot, and she started rearranging bottles in an already neat supply closet.

"Are you saying that wasn't real?"

Dallas turned to face her. "Well, I—"

"Dallas Wade, you've fallen for the guy. It's written all over you. Go ahead and blather on if you want, but there's a look in your eye that definitely wasn't there yesterday. And from the way he just kissed you, I'd say it's a mutual attraction."

Dallas's shoulders sagged. "I don't know, Amber. I think I'm in over my head."

"You?" Amber's brown eyes sparkled. "Must have been quite a night."

Dallas felt her flush returning.

"I just knew it!" Amber crowed. "There's something about the way he carries himself that practically shouts what a good lover he'd be. Have you noticed how he draws women to him? He could have anyone in this place, but you snagged him. Good going, girl."

Dallas sank back onto the arm of the swivel chair. "I could be making the biggest mistake of my life. He's a bounty hunter, Amber. A soldier of fortune. He ad-mitted he lives for adventure. He's probably attracted to me because I have Neal Parnell following me around. Once I'm not in danger, I'll be dull and boring and he'll move on."

Amber gazed at her thoughtfully. "And I take it that would bother you?"

"That's what's scaring me. I don't want him getting to me like that."

"I think he already has."

"Life used to be so simple." Dallas rubbed her forehead. "I used to know exactly what I wanted—to own a business, maybe even franchise someday, live in the country and raise purebred dogs. If the right guy came along, he'd be icing on the cake."

"And not the main ingredient in the batter."

"Exactly." Dallas glanced up at her. "I swore I'd never be that vulnerable. We hear it in country songs all the time—'I'm nothing without you,' 'I can't live without you,' and on and on. I hate that idea."

"But love can make you feel that way," Amber said gently.

Dallas skipped away from the word, but it kept flashing like neon in her mind. "Then who needs it?" she said finally in frustration. "Why trade our independence for an emotion that puts us at the mercy of some guy who will probably run off and leave us?"

Amber put down her manicure tray and sat in a chair opposite Dallas. "This is partly my fault. I told you to ask Gabe about your problem. Sure, I thought you two might get it on, but you always seem to handle things so well. I thought if anything you'd be the one to break his heart. I guess I never imagined you getting hurt. I'm sorry."

Dallas smile felt forced. "I'm a big girl. I didn't have to go to bed with him."

"If I'd been in your shoes, I would have. He's gorgeous, Dallas. I don't blame you for flipping out. But what if you're wrong about him? Maybe he'll end up making a commitment."

"Amber, he told me he won't even keep a dog because of his life-style."

"Oh." She frowned. "I see your point." Then she turned and glanced toward the pool tables where Gabe whipped a cue stick forward, scattering balls in a powerful break. His back to Amber and Dallas, he leaned across the table for his next shot. Amber sighed. "Nice buns."

Dallas looked away from the tempting sight of Gabe's backside. "I'm well aware of that fact."

"What are you going to do?"

"Cut some hair." Dallas pushed herself up from the chair. "We have customers approaching."

THE NIGHT SEEMED endless. Thankfully Neal was totally engrossed in Beth, so Dallas didn't have to deal with him. His preoccupation with the waitress made it seem even less likely that he'd been the prowler who had set Gretchen off the night before.

About ten o'clock the stream of customers had slackened off, and despite all her misgivings about their relationship, Dallas longed to be with Gabe. She glanced out to where he sat at the bar, an untouched mug of beer in front of him. Apparently he'd been watching her, because he raised his glass in salute before taking a sip.

"Take a break and go see him," Amber said.

"Yeah, that will sure help."

"Go see him. People change their minds about things. And whether you want to be or not, you're hooked, so why not spend time with the guy?" She gave Dallas a little push toward the door. "Go on."

"I suppose." Dallas adjusted her hat and walked toward the bar.

Gabe watched her approach, his dark eyes glinting, a small smile on his face.

"You haven't been out on the floor tonight," she said as she drew near. As busy as she'd been, she'd kept track of him, and although the usual number of women had asked him to dance, he'd turned them all down, to her immense satisfaction.

"I've been waiting for you," he said, rising from the stool.

"Oh, well, I didn't mean that we—" She realized a line dance had begun. "Do you know this?"

"You can teach me."

When she hesitated, he took her hand and led her to the floor.

Dallas knew the song and the dance, which was why she'd hesitated. The song was about making love, and the dance—the Tush Push—included suggestive hip movements to match the words. But Gabe was already lining up with the other dancers, and she had to coach him or they'd be run over.

"Like this," she demonstrated. Gabe stuck his thumbs through his belt loops and followed with the fluid movement that had carried them through the magical waltz. But this dance was a different story. She got him through the kicks and foot stomps. "Now pump your hips like this."

He imitated her perfectly, and her mouth went dry at the sight of his lean hips moving in the rhythm that

had brought her such pleasure hours before. A dancer
bumped into her as she stood staring at him.

She quickly got back in step, and then realized Gabe
had slid to the next movement without being told.

"You knew this already!"

He grinned and continued the dance. "I liked the way
you demonstrated it," he said as they whirled into the
next phase.

"That's unfair!"

"All's fair in love and war." He spun away from her.
And which is this? The music pounded at her. Love.
Love. Love.

They moved in perfect synchronization. His body
lured her with every swing of his hips, and she paid him
back in full with suggestive rotations of her own. Each
time he caught her glance, his eyes promised that this
was only a prelude to what they'd enjoy later. Her
blood pumped in time with the staccato beat of the
music as the lyrics asked when they would be making
love. *Soon*, said his eyes. *Soon*, she silently replied.

She was so involved that she almost missed seeing
Neal standing by the rail surrounding the dance floor.
But Gabe didn't miss him. She saw his body stiffen as
his gaze locked with Neal's. Gabe didn't miss a step, but
Dallas could sense the power of that single glance, feel
the hate pulsing between the two men. Then Neal
turned his head, and his blue eyes blazed as he glared
at her.

In an instant the sexy dance took on a sinister tone.
The fun of taunting Gabe vanished as she realized Neal
had been watching every sensuous move. He gripped

the rail, his jaw clenched and his full lips curled in disdain.

"I have to get back," Dallas said and left the floor, sick dread curdling in her stomach.

CAUTION AND CONTROL had guided Dallas her entire life, yet she couldn't grasp the concepts now. When Gabe took the truck keys from her as they walked to the parking lot that night she relinquished them and allowed him to drive home. When his hand reached for hers across the seat, she slid her fingers unresistingly through his.

Lord help her, she was starting to weave fantasies that included Gabe. Sure, his marriage had ended because his wife was too dependent and now he lived like a vagabond who didn't seem to want any ties, but as Amber said, people change.

In the darkness, with only the dashboard lights illuminating their faces, she felt easier about probing a little more into his life. "Do you . . . have any family in Tucson?"

"Just my sister." His answer was short, but not unfriendly.

"Your folks live somewhere else, then?"

"No, they're dead."

"Oh, Gabe, I'm sorry. There I go again, butting in."

He squeezed her hand. "It's been ten years."

She wanted to ask how they'd died, but didn't have the nerve.

After a brief silence, he continued. "It wasn't very pretty. Some guy'd been arrested for a hit and run, and he posted bail. Then he took off, but his car quit on

him, and he flagged down my folks on the highway."
His fingers tightened, but his voice remained steady.
"My dad was the type to stop and help anybody. They
gave him a lift. He directed them off into the desert, shot
them and took off with their truck."

"That's horrible."

"A bounty hunter helped track him down. I went to
thank the guy and learned a lot about bail enforcement. Seemed like a hell of a lot better job than digging
stuff out of the ground."

She took his clenched hand in both of hers. "That
explains a lot."

"Oh, I don't know." His hand relaxed in hers. "I
suppose a shrink would say I've been avenging my
parents ever since. That might have been part of it at
first, but the truth is, I was bored with working in the
mine, and I love this job. I couldn't go back to a regular routine for all the gold in China."

Or all the love in my heart? She hit the wall of reality once again. How many times did he have to warn
her that he was an untamable rogue before she finally
started to listen?

GABE HAD BEEN EXPECTING the question about his family. A cautious woman like Dallas would want to know
a guy's background before she got too involved with
him. She might even have some crazy idea he'd give up
his job if she asked him to. But if she wanted him, she'd
have to take him as he was. He didn't think there was
much chance she'd do that, but he'd always been drawn
by a long shot.

If she'd give up her notion that all of life fit into neat little compartments, they might, just might, be able to build something together. For now he was satisfied with little victories, like that spontaneous lovemaking session today and convincing her to kiss him at Rowdy Ranch.

He wished she'd take Parnell more seriously, but apparently the scumball wouldn't come around as long as Gabe was in residence. That was okay. He liked being in residence. Probably liked it more than was good for him.

"I don't think Parnell followed us out here," he said as he disengaged his hand to swing the truck into its parking space. "I've been checking the mirror, and no black Corvette showed up. Not that he couldn't drive out later, but I doubt he will."

"He seems pretty involved with Beth."

"Don't be fooled by that." He turned off the engine. "A guy like Parnell gets tired of a woman who makes a conquest too easy for him."

She gave him a smile that made his heart feel tight in his chest. "How about you? Do you get tired of a woman when there's no challenge?"

He wanted to take her right there, on the seat of the truck. Tired of her? Not in a million years. "I'm not like Parnell," he said, climbing down from the cab. The vision of seeing her naked on the rumpled sheets of her bed made him tremble as he helped her down from the truck and opened the gate.

"Watch out for Gretchen," she warned, grabbing the dog's collar.

He shoved the gate closed behind him and took her hand. "I must admit Gretchen's not my top priority right now."

She got that shy, excited note in her voice that he loved. "Maybe I should leave Gretchen out in the yard for a little while."

"I think that's an excellent idea." That hesitant sexiness of hers made him want to beat his chest and yell out a warning to any male within ten miles that this was his territory. A primitive reaction, and one he wouldn't admit to her, but true, nevertheless.

"I'll get her lighted collar, so I can see she's okay out here."

She could get a rhinestone overcoat for the dog as far as he was concerned. Just so she did it in a hurry.

The three of them went in the front door and Gabe took off his jacket and hat while Dallas opened a drawer in the kitchen and took out a studded collar. She buckled it around Gretchen's neck and flicked a small switch. Gabe shook his head in amazement. What had looked to be studs were really little red lights that blinked in sequence, like a Las Vegas sign.

"There." Dallas opened the door and Gretchen bounded back out, her collar signaling her whereabouts even though the darkness swallowed her up. Dallas closed the door and glanced out the window. "I feel better when I can see where she is."

He admired the way her denim shorts cupped her firm bottom. "That's not exactly what would make me feel better."

"Oh?" She turned, a gleam in her gray eyes. Then she took off her hat and combed her fingers back through her hair. "And what would make you feel better, cowboy?"

He stared at her, mute with need.

With a soft chuckle she hung her hat by the door. Turning back to him, she removed her fringed jacket with deliberate slowness, rolling her shoulders back to peel off each sleeve in a gesture that thrust her breasts forward against the white cotton of her shirt.

His mouth went dry, his palms grew moist. This demand to lie with her was growing greater, not less. "Why do I always feel as if it's been weeks?"

"Einstein said time is relative." She began unfastening her shirt one slow button after another.

He stepped toward her. "He must have been watching you undress."

"Impatient, Gabe?" She arched her eyebrows, obviously reveling in her power.

"Not me." He forced himself to stop, to leave his arms at his sides. "An impatient guy would never have made it through all those shampoos, all those haircuts, where you ran your fingers through other guys' hair. Then there was that line dance while you wiggled your tush right in front of me."

"As if you weren't doing the same," she retorted, but her lips parted and her breathing quickened. He'd evened the balance of power.

"Then I waited through the interminable balancing of the cash register receipts," he said. "There was a tiny drop of perspiration that slid down between your breasts while you were totaling the final figures. An impatient guy might have torn your shirt off and licked that little drop away, but I didn't."

She swayed, and he closed the gap between them. She filled his arms as no woman ever had. The blood roared in his ears. She arched against him as his mouth found hers; his tongue plunged into the soft, moist—
She began struggling, and he held her tighter. What was wrong? Why was she trying to get away from him?

"Gretchen's barking," she said, breathless as she pulled free.

He shook his head to clear it. The dog *was* barking. He stepped to the side of the window and glanced out. Dallas's dusk-to-dawn light illuminated the huge shape of the Saint Bernard—wolfhound mix outside the fence. "It's lover boy," he said. "Probably thinks this is the red-light district."

"Very funny." Dallas joined him by the window, her hand holding her shirt together in front. "Let's shoo him away. He makes me nervous."

"I'll do it." He started toward the door just as he heard a metal clinking sound. Dumb dogs were probably trying to push through the fence. The sound came again.

"Gabe, did you latch the gate tight?"

"I just pushed it closed. I thought it latched by itself." He hadn't been thinking much about gates at the time.

Dallas raced for the door and flung it open. "She's out!" she called as she ran down the steps and across the yard.

He tore off after her. Sure enough, far down the road bounded a pair of large dogs, red blinking lights merrily advertising the direction of their flight.

Gabe overtook Dallas and passed her. The dogs had romped into the middle of a field, and before he could get to them, the new motion of the red lights and the fevered whining told him what was happening to Gretchen. A wail from behind him told him Dallas knew it, too.

Gretchen had lost her virginity.

10

"WE HAVE TO GET THEM apart," Dallas said, shoving past him. "Igor! Stop that!"

"Hold on." Gabe grabbed her and pulled her back. "Igor will tear you to bits if you try to interrupt his pleasure at this point."

"I suppose you'd know," she said, sounding disgusted with all males and their propensities.

"I have some idea how he feels right now. It's too late, anyway. You know that."

"Damn!" She watched a moment longer as the dogs coupled enthusiastically. Then she turned away with a groan. "That gate has to be latched carefully, Gabe. You can't just shove it closed, because the little latch doesn't always come down."

He didn't like her subtle accusation, but understood she was upset. "Then I guess it needs some oil."

"Well, I've been a little *busy* to oil gate latches, okay?"

"Don't blame me." Well, she was getting to him, after all. She could stir him to anger, just as she could stir him to passion. He shouldn't be surprised. "I tried like hell to stay out of your bed," he reminded her.

"Oh, sure!" She spread her arms, which made her unbuttoned blouse gape open. He tried not to look and let his anger dilute. He failed.

"What was I supposed to do, with you sleeping right in the next room?" she shouted. "Do you think I'm some robot? Some creature made of some space-age material that doesn't get hot when some guy with a body to die for is standing in the doorway of her bedroom and—"

"You really think I have a body to die for?" He couldn't stay angry with somebody throwing out compliments like that.

"It's very nice!" She sounded quite upset about it. "Are you satisfied now, Mr. Egomaniac?"

"Not by a long shot." He worked not to smile. "But I think he is." Gabe gestured toward the male dog, who had stopped moving and now drooped across Gretchen's rump. "Maybe I should offer them each a cigarette."

"How cute." Dallas glanced over her shoulder. "Can you imagine what the puppies will look like?"

"You never know. They might have bodies to die for." He couldn't keep the laughter out of his voice.

She rounded on him. "You think this is so funny, don't you? My whole breeding program is down the tubes. And I'm sure this isn't good for Gretchen."

"In the long run, maybe not, but short-term I'm sure it was very good for Gretchen."

"Oh!" She threw both hands in the air. "Is that all you can think about? If you hadn't been so engrossed in sex a little while ago, none of this would have happened."

"Excuse me? Are you saying you weren't at all excited yourself?" He stared pointedly at her unbuttoned blouse. "Or was that the work of mysterious forces beyond your control?"

She glanced down. "Oh." Then she began rebuttoning her blouse, keeping her chin down so she didn't have to look at him. By the time she finished, Igor had wandered off and Gretchen stood beside her, tongue hanging out and tail wagging. Dallas hooked a couple of fingers through Gretchen's collar and started down the road.

Falling into step beside her, Gabe decided to offer no more excuses or explanations. Maybe that was it between him and Dallas. If she chose to end their relationship because of this incident with the dog, then he hadn't made any progress whatsoever, and it was just as well they parted now. He'd still make sure Parnell didn't attack her, but he could do that without being in her house and in her bed.

"I don't like it when things don't go the way I planned," she said at last.

He remained silent, waiting.

"I shouldn't have blamed you. It was as much my fault as yours. More, really."

The tenseness in his gut loosened. "I'm willing to share equally," he said, his tone mild.

"Well, you're not equally to blame. It's my gate, my dog and my responsibility to see that the dog stays on the right side of the gate."

"Not if I'm part of your life. Then the responsibility's shared."

"Not if I don't wish to share it."

His insides twisted. "Is that the way you want things to be, then?" They'd reached his truck. He still had his keys in his pocket. She could send him his jacket.

She glanced up at him, her face pale in the dusk-to-dawn light. "I don't know, Gabe."

It wasn't really a call for a truce, but he'd take it. They were beating around the issues, but he didn't feel ready to hit them head-on yet. Did they have a future? What compromises were each of them willing to make toward that future? He didn't have the answers, and he didn't think she did, either. But he ached to hold her again. That much, at least, was simple.

"Let's get Gretchen inside and make sure she's okay," he said, reaching for the latch on the gate.

She accepted the suggestion quickly. It seemed she didn't want deep discussions right now any more than he did. Maybe the sizzling chemistry between them was enough to take them through a few more days, until they both decided how much they were willing to sacrifice for this fragile relationship blossoming between them.

They ushered a subdued Gretchen into the house. After checking her over and finding no bites or scratches, Dallas snapped off the switch on the blinking collar and unbuckled it from Gretchen's neck. As she hung it on a hook by the door, Dallas's shoulders started to shake.

Gabe felt instant remorse for making fun of Gretchen's night out. He hurried over and took her by the shoulders. "Don't cry. I'm sure everything will be okay."

She turned in his arms, her eyes sparkling with amusement, not tears. "Gretchen looked so *dumb*, standing there with that collar blinking away, while

Igor—" She lost the rest of her sentence to the laughter that spilled out of her like warm rain.

He grinned. "Can't say I've ever seen a show like that myself."

"I suppose..." She stopped and giggled again. "I suppose the collar would have been more appropriate wound around her tail."

"I don't think Igor needed any more directions. He found the target just fine."

"I'll bet he's one happy dog tonight."

Gabe molded his hands around her bottom. "Poor old Igor. He must have trouble finding a lover that fits. And he'll never have that kind of satisfaction with Gretchen again."

"Not if I can help it." She nestled against him, her gray eyes turning smoky as he massaged her buttocks.

"Heartless woman." His sex swelled beneath his jeans. She could bring him to the brink of desperation so fast it was scary.

"Oh, I wouldn't say that." She reached her arms around his neck and stood on tiptoe to brush her lips against his.

Desire thickened his vocal chords. "Prove it."

She slid out of his arms and turned to the dog. "Gretchen, lie down." Gretchen plopped to the floor and put her head on her paws. "Stay," Dallas instructed. Then she turned back to Gabe and crooked one finger.

At that moment he would have followed her anywhere.

Once inside the bedroom, she closed the door and leaned against it to take off her boots. Then, while he watched in an increasing state of arousal, she discarded her shirt and fringed shorts, until she stood before him in thong-style panties and a tease of a bra.

She motioned him toward the bed. "We'll start with your boots." Straddling his leg, she presented an enticing view of her backside as she pulled off his boot with practiced ease.

He ran a finger down her spine. "Seems like you might have done this maneuver before." He considered himself liberated when it came to former lovers, but he didn't feel liberated when he contemplated Dallas taking off another guy's boots.

"Yep." She stepped over his other leg and repeated the process. Then she turned and sat astride his lap. He started to reach for her, but she grabbed his wrists. "You have a problem with that, cowboy?"

"Yes." The word was out before he could call it back.

"Too bad." Still astride him, she released his wrists and placed both hands on his chest. He allowed her to push him down to the mattress. Then she began unbuttoning his shirt, her hair falling around her face and over her scantily covered breasts. "I've had hundreds of lovers," she said, rocking gently against his groin.

"Liar." He dug his fingers into her soft bottom.

"How do you know?" She scooted back just enough to unbuckle his belt.

"You think all Dave Fogarty and I do is play pool?" He gasped as she unbuttoned his jeans and reached in to stroke his bulging manhood. "He's told me all about you. Engaged once. Didn't work out. You don't even— Damn, that feels good—" He groaned as she slipped her hand inside his briefs.

"I don't even what?"

"Go out much." He closed his eyes in ecstasy.

"Maybe I lied to Dave." She paused in her fondling and braced her hands on either side of his head so she could lean down and nibble on his lower lip. "And why did you want to know, anyway?"

He grasped her by the waist and in one deft movement rolled over, sending her sprawling underneath him on the bed. "Lord knows why," he said, panting from excitement and the exertion of changing positions. "I certainly didn't expect to find a twenty-nine-year-old virgin in this day and age. Not one who looks like you, anyway. But damned if I like the idea of any other guy, even one, being inside you."

Her gray eyes glowed. "That's being a bit possessive, Escalante."

"I know." He admired the way her breasts heaved beneath him. "Was he good? The guy you were engaged to?"

She licked her lips. "Great."

"Damn you." He kissed her hard, thrusting his tongue deep into her mouth. When he'd opened the front fastening of her bra he plundered her breasts, nipping with his teeth at her soft flesh. There may have been other lovers, but he was here now, and she would never forget him. Never.

She writhed beneath him, arching her hips upward until he reached down and pulled away the damp scrap of cotton between her legs. He resented the delay while he put on a condom. Finally he buried himself in her warm, moist center. There. He pushed forward a little more and felt her ripple of reaction rise up and enfold him.

"You're mine now," he murmured, drawing back and easing forward again, locking in on the center of her response. She quivered once again. "Mine." He didn't move much. He didn't need to. She was trembling all over now, a volatile mixture ready to erupt all around him. He pressed forward insistently—seeking, seeking. Her trembling grew more violent. His voice was hoarse as he repeated the word. His teeth raked across her throat. *Mine.*

Then, with one final push he tapped into the epicenter of her passion, and her cry of affirmation rang in his ears. As her spasms guided him to his own shattering release, he accepted a truth his body had known since the first time he'd lain with her. She was his . . . and he was hers.

SHE'D WANTED TO BE claimed. She couldn't deny it, all her feminist rhetoric to the contrary. When he'd demanded her allegiance, she'd had no choice but to grant it. That didn't give him the right to tell her what to do. That didn't give him dominion over her life. But it gave him her loyalty and her fidelity.

Perhaps she'd known from the beginning that he could wrest such a promise from her, and she'd feared the power that implied. In the end, it was an easy promise to make. How could she ever welcome another into her bed after experiencing such total communion with Gabe?

Still breathing hard, he raised his head to look into her eyes, as if searching for confirmation. Without speaking, she met his gaze.

His breath caught, and he swallowed. "Once I told a woman that I loved her," he began. "What I felt was a soft emotion. Sweet. And so...*pale* compared to this." He touched her cheek. "I don't know what this is."

"Neither do I."

"I thought maybe..." He smoothed a strand of hair back from her cheek as he seemed to grope for words. "Maybe it was just plain old lust." His wry smile squeezed her heart. "But I've lusted after centerfolds in magazines, and I never had the urge to— This will really sound chauvinistic—I want to *brand* you somehow, so that no man will ever even think about the prospect of having you." His voice dropped to a husky whisper. "He'd have to kill me first."

Stirred by his intensity, she cradled his face in her hands. "You're right. That's not very politically correct."

"But it's honestly the way I feel."

She met his gaze, all pretense stripped away. "That's how I feel about you. Any woman who wants you has to get past me. And, Gabe, I fibbed about the man I was engaged to. He doesn't hold a candle to you." She paused. "No one does."

"That's good, because your days of experimenting are over."

She decided to go for broke. "Do you realize what you're saying?"

"Yes." His eyes smiled into hers, bringing joy surging through her. "Which doesn't mean all the rough parts are worked out of this arrangement," he cautioned. "It just means they will be."

"You sound so sure."

He shrugged. "It's simple, really. I can't stand the idea of someone else making love to you. You're a vibrant, healthy woman with lots of years of lovemaking ahead of you. So if I'm ruling out anybody else satisfying you, I guess the job falls to me."

"What a noble sacrifice," she said, laughing.

"Isn't it, though?" He leaned down and kissed her softly. "I need you, *mi querida*."

"Oh, Gabe." She savored the gentle message conveyed by his kiss. Maybe they could make it, after all.

They held each other in contented silence for long moments. Finally he propped his head on his fist and gazed at her. "How about some refrozen ice cream? I'm starved."

"Not me. But you go ahead."

"Thanks, I will." He rolled away from her and stood. "You're sure? I'll bring it to you."

"No, thanks." She levered herself up and watched him pull on his jeans and shirt. "I use that ice cream for comfort food when things aren't going well."

He glanced at her. "Since you had me pick it up this morning, I guess you anticipated needing some comfort."

"I wasn't sure what would happen between us."

"I'm still not sure." He leaned down and gave her a quick kiss. "But that's okay. Come on in and keep me company while I eat the ice cream."

She grabbed a robe from the closet. By the time she entered the kitchen he was already scooping ice cream into the mug that said Hair Stylists Get You All Lath-ered Up. Gretchen stood close by, looking hopeful.

"Couldn't find a bowl?" she asked, leaning against a cupboard.

"I've been wanting to use this mug ever since last night."

"Was it only last night?"

He stopped scooping and turned to her. "Yeah, in-credible as that seems." Then he continued filling the mug.

She could hardly believe that the same man who had stood in her kitchen and seemed so remote the night before could be the same guy who stood barefoot in front of her sink, his shirt hanging open, his hair tou-sled from their lovemaking. "What a difference a day makes."

He winked at her. "That's for sure." Then he tossed the scoop in the sink and took a spoon out of a drawer.

"I usually give Gretchen a little in her bowl."

"Okay." He picked up the scoop, dug out a generous portion and flicked it into Gretchen's bowl. She im-mediately lowered her head and started lapping. Then he returned the scoop to the sink and put away the ice cream.

Dallas started over to rinse the scoop and put it in the dishwasher.

Gabe caught her eye just as she reached for the scoop. "Why not leave it?" he asked casually.

"Because I usually don't."

"I tend to leave things around."

She held his gaze. "I tend to put them away."

"Hmm." He regarded her thoughtfully, as if she were an experiment he was working on. "Maybe we'll have to have separate houses."

"Isn't that a little extreme? You could make a greater effort to pick things up."

"Or you could learn to leave them lying around." The corners of his mouth twitched. "Oh, the arguments we'll have, Dallas."

She gazed at him in astonishment. "You sound as if you relish the arguing."

"Arguing's not so bad."

"It's not?"

"Nope. Keeps things exciting." He leaned against the counter and scooped out some ice cream. Her gaze lingered with appreciation on the expanse of hair-sprinkled chest revealed each time he took another bite. "After all, you have to argue before you can make up."

She sank to a kitchen chair in bewilderment. "I thought the idea was to find somebody you could agree with most of the time."

"So did I. Then I met you. I know for a fact we won't agree on lots of things, but I have to be with you, so the arguing will be part of it, I guess." He gestured to the ice cream with his spoon. "This isn't bad refrozen."

He wasn't bad, either, she thought. The soft jeans molded the lines of his crotch, lines she could now trace in her mind's eye from memory. She propped her chin on one hand. "We wouldn't have to argue all the time, you know. You could just give in."

"That's not in my nature."

"No kidding."

"It's not in yours, either," he said around another scoop of ice cream. "Don't sweat it, Dallas."

"Two days ago I wouldn't have believed anyone who told me I'd be having this conversation."

"Two days ago we hadn't made love."

"Good point." How she loved to look at him. Even the movement of the muscle in his forearm when he lifted the spoon made her stomach tighten with desire.

"Although saying it's only been a short time is deceiving." He scraped his spoon around the bottom of the mug. "We've been working on this attraction a lot longer than two days. It all started with that shampoo."

"I beg your pardon. I treated you the way I treat every customer."

"Is that right?" He took a chair across from her and set the mug and spoon in front of him. "Then it was my imagination that you fondled my hair a little more than necessary?"

She flushed. "Well, maybe I—"

"And the way you leaned over me. I swear I could almost read your mind, and you were thinking of something more than washing my hair."

"Nonsense."

"Really?" He took the spoon from the mug. Droplets of melted ice cream clung to it. He reached for her hand and held the spoon over her wrist until a trickle of ice cream fell with a cool plop on her pulse point. "I'll admit to you that I was imagining how your fingers would feel on other parts of my body." He lifted her wrist and licked the ice cream away, sending a tingling shot of awareness through her body to settle in that sweet, aching spot he'd so recently turned into a volcano of sensation. "Fess up, Dallas."

She struggled to remain calm. "You're arrogant, Escalante. You think every woman is hot for your body."

"I don't care about every woman." He dribbled more ice cream in the crook of her arm. "I want to know if you were." He lowered his lips to her arm. "That first night."

"Maybe." The cool ice cream followed by the warmth of his mouth was driving her crazy with desire.

"Just maybe?" he prompted, dripping ice cream into her palm.

"All right. Yes."

"And now?" He circled her palm with his tongue and followed the tiny rivulets of ice cream that had oozed between her fingers.

She was embarrassed by the ease with which he could arouse her. She turned her face away. "Gabe, we just—"

He put down the spoon and caught her chin to bring her back to face him. "Ah, Dallas, don't hide from me. That's what I wanted to see. The need in those beautiful gray eyes." Still holding her hand, he stood and came around the table. "Come here, *mi querida*."

The soft Spanish endearment swept away whatever small resistance she had. She allowed him to pull her to her feet and open her robe. Reaching behind her for the mug, he guided her up against the table. He slowly dripped more ice cream over her breasts and licked them clean until she was panting with need. Then he kneeled before her, and the last of the cool liquid found its way to her heated center. She groaned, shameless now, all inhibitions gone as he replaced the coolness with his tongue.

When she thought she could take no more, he rose and unfastened the fly of his jeans. A condom appeared in his hand, although she was past caring if he used one. The table edge bit into her backside as he thrust forward, but she didn't care about that, either. He provided enough pleasure to make her forget everything else.

He cradled her face as he moved easily within her. "I love you," he said, his voice hoarse. "I love you, Dallas."

Tears of happiness filled her eyes. "I love you, Gabe."

"Forever." He kissed her as she shuddered in his arms. Then with a muffled groan he found his own release.

GABE WASN'T HAPPY when he saw the small bruises on Dallas's bottom as she toweled off after their shower the next morning.

He pulled her over to the bed where he'd sat to pull on his boots. "We can't have this happening," he said, bending to inspect the marks. "We'll have to get all our furniture padded."

"I kind of like them. They're like the brand you talked about wanting to put on me." She laughed as his lips tickled over the bruises. "Every time I sit down today I'll think of you."

"I'd rather have a different reminder than that." He released her and reached for his shirt. "And I thought you wanted to go riding today. Can you?"

She gave him a look of scorn as she stepped into her panties. "I'm no hothouse flower. I believe I told you that."

"Yeah, that was when I discovered you had a gun. That set me back some. Which reminds me, I should call Diego and Jasper, find out what Parnell's been up to recently."

Dallas snapped the front catch on her bra. "You still have them following him?"

"Not every minute, but they're keeping track of him. Why?"

"Because I think it's silly, that's why." She pulled a T-shirt over her head. "He's not doing anything wrong."

"You have a short memory," Gabe said, buttoning his shirt and standing to tuck it into his jeans. "What about the times he followed you? What about Friday night? If I weren't around, you'd be in hot water, lady."

His tone sent her hackles up. She paused in the act of reaching for her jeans. "I think you're exaggerating the situation."

After all they'd shared, she didn't think he'd react with the same closed-down expression as before. She was wrong. "Gabe, for heaven's sake, what is it? Why do you get this way?"

He shoved his hands in his pockets and gazed out the window.

"Dammit, what aren't you telling me about Neal? There's more to this, isn't there?"

He seemed to be struggling with whether to confide in her or not. Whatever thoughts he had, they were obviously painful.

A horrible suspicion arose in her mind. She tossed the jeans aside and walked over to lay a hand on his arm. "Gabe, is Neal related to that man who killed your parents?"

He shook his head and glanced down at her. Then he looked away again. His words, when they finally came, were filled with fury. "Neal Parnell raped my sister."

11

DALLAS HUGGED HERSELF against the sudden chill that engulfed her. She stared at Gabe, who kept his back to her, his head bowed. "Your sister is Celia Martinez?" she asked, her voice little more than a whisper.

He nodded.

"Oh, Gabe. Why didn't you tell me?"

"Because I thought it would make you question my judgment about Parnell."

"I've been questioning it, anyway." And now she doubted he had any objectivity at all. Her heart ached—for him, for her, for the tender emotions that had been created between them and now seemed in jeopardy. She forced herself to say the words. "You weren't at the trial."

His jaw clenched. "I didn't have to be. Celia told me he did it. That's enough for me."

"But the evidence—"

He whirled, his expression dangerous. "Damn the evidence! She *knows* it was him. And you would, too, if you weren't so caught up in the details! Everything has to be lined up and neat for you, doesn't it?"

She had to grit her teeth to keep them from chattering. "That's how the system works."

"That's what I'm trying to tell you. It didn't work."

"It did! He had a fair trial. I agree he's not the most appetizing guy to have around, and I've gone along with you and Amber because I didn't like the way he seemed to be fixating on me. But twelve intelligent people studied the evidence at that trial. He did not commit that rape."

"Like hell."

They stood as if a ten-foot wall separated them. And perhaps it did, she thought. They were never going to agree on this. And it was no longer a philosophical discussion, as she'd thought before. His narrowed eyes and the arrogant tilt of his head told her he was in full warrior mode again. Her stomach churned as she realized what she had to do.

"You're sure he's a rapist and his next target is me, right?"

"I'd bet my life on it."

"But he seems to have backed off now that you're around all the time."

"That's right. I could have protected Celia, too, if I'd been here. But I wasn't. That's something I'll have to live with for the rest of my life."

Anguish tore at her. Was his devotion to her only a salve for his guilty conscience about his sister? She couldn't believe that or she'd go completely crazy. She took a deep breath. "We can prove your premise. All you have to do is leave."

His head snapped as if she'd hit him across the face. His jaw worked, and when he spoke his voice was strained. "I can't leave the way open for him to hurt you."

"Then we'll never know who's right, will we?"

His gaze grew icy cold. "Do you want me to go?"

It was the hardest word she'd ever had to say. "Yes."

All emotion left his face. "All right."

"You're wrong about Neal. He won't come after me."

His tone was almost conversational, and all the more chilling because of that. "Let's hope not. Because I'd have to kill him."

DALLAS SPENT THE DAY riding in the foothills until Sugar was lathered and the tears soaking Dallas's T-shirt had dried in the warm sun. She stayed away from the trailer as long as possible, but eventually she had to go back to the rumpled sheets, the damned sticky mug and spoon still on the table and the rest of the coffee ice cream. She'd never be able to use it as comfort food again.

She threw out the ice cream. If Amber hadn't given her the mug, she'd have thrown it away, too, rather than rinse it out. But Amber loved that mug and used it every time she came over. Fresh tears streamed down Dallas's cheeks and she used water hot enough to hurt her hands as she cleaned the mug and spoon. The least he could have done was rinse his own damned dishes!

Thoughts of Amber reminded Dallas that she needed to explain the changed situation before she and Amber worked together again. She called and made a lunch date for the next day.

"What? You can tear yourself away from that gorgeous hunk for a lunch with little ol' me?" Amber asked.

"Anytime," Dallas said, forcing cheer into her voice.

"Want to go shopping, too?"

"Maybe."

"I'll bet you need some new underwear. I always get new underwear when I start a relationship. This will be fun, Dallas, having you two as a couple."

Dallas gripped the phone and tried to think of how to stop Amber from babbling on.

"I think Vince and Gabe might get along," Amber continued. "Maybe the four of us can go out together sometime."

Dallas grabbed at the first thing she could think of. "Oh, God, I think I left the gate open, Amber. Gretchen might get out."

"Oh, no! Can't have that."

"Right. See you tomorrow." She hung up and gazed at the phone through her tears. Gabe had certainly messed up her life. Even her dog wasn't the same.

But she could do something about Igor. She dialed the number of her neighbor who owned the dog. "Mr. Stanhope? This is Dallas Wade down the road. I suggest you either get Igor neutered or keep him penned up. If I see him on my property again I'm taking him to the Humane Society."

"What happened? Did he compromise that pretty little Great Dane of yours?" Stanhope laughed.

"Mr. Stanhope, I'm warning you. It's irresponsible to allow an unneutered dog to run around impregnating the world."

Stanhope laughed even louder. "Hell, that dog of yours is the only one he can reach. Any of the other females in the neighborhood would have to agree to stand on a stool."

"Mr. Stanhope—"

"Ease up, Dallas. I'll help you find homes for the puppies, if that's your problem."

"No, that's not my problem, and please keep your dog penned up!" She put the phone down with more force than necessary and stomped out to feed the horses their evening meal.

As the shadows lengthened in the yard, she found herself glancing down the road. If a black Corvette showed up...but of course it wouldn't. Neal would probably spend the night at Rowdy Ranch, and tonight was Amber's night to work alone, so Dallas wouldn't have to risk seeing him—or Gabe.

Maybe she'd spend the night watching television. She hardly ever gave herself time to do that. And she'd lock all the doors and windows. Not that she really needed to. Gabe was so determined to find his sister's attacker and punish him that he couldn't see that Neal was innocent.

"Come on, Gretchen." She took the dog by the collar and went inside, locking the door firmly behind her.

The sound of the television kept her company all evening. She ate a microwaved dinner in front of it, and if she didn't like the current show she switched over to the country-music video station. When the video for "A Cowboy's Dream" came on, she channel surfed until she found a sitcom that made her laugh.

"Television's good," she murmured to herself. "I'll watch more television."

On one of her forays through the stations a courtroom drama caught her attention. The judge was in her chambers discussing some point of law with the prosecuting attorney.

"I'm sorry, but that's not admissable," the judge told the attorney.

The prosecutor looked about ready to explode. "But it proves the defendant murdered his wife."

"Nevertheless, you and I know it's not admissable. If you enter it, I'll have to declare a mistrial, and I know you don't want that, either. Prove your case without this evidence. You're a good enough attorney."

But he didn't, and Dallas's attention was riveted to the set as the supposed murderer went free because the jury never learned about the damning evidence. She switched to another channel, but the courtroom drama stayed with her.

That was only television, she told herself. How dramatic to have unusable evidence that would convict a killer. That probably happened once in a million times. She and the jury had heard everything there was to hear about the Celia Martinez case. Of course they had.

She didn't sleep well that night and got up three times to recheck the locks on her doors and windows.

DALLAS MET AMBER at an Italian restaurant near the bustling Tucson Mall. They'd both dressed in slacks and sweaters; lunching out for them had always meant getting away from cowgirl clothes for a few hours.

Dallas saved her announcement until after the waiter had deposited a large all-you-can-eat salad bowl and two salad plates on their table. Then she told Amber what had happened, even including the incident with Gretchen.

"You sent that man away?" Amber wailed, her fork clattering to her salad plate. "You are out of your mind, girl."

"He's paranoid, Amber." Dallas picked up a green chili pepper by the stem and put it back on her plate. She wasn't hungry. "I can understand it, I guess. If your sister swears some guy raped her, then you want to believe she's right, so you can have somebody to hang the hate on."

"Dallas, look at me."

Dallas lifted her head.

"Has it ever occurred to you that—now don't get mad at me—that maybe, just maybe, Neal was guilty of that charge?"

Dallas gazed at her as snippets from the television courtroom drama played in her mind. "But the evidence didn't support—"

"I know you hate the idea that you might have turned a rapist loose."

Dallas shook her head. "I didn't. And the other eleven people on that jury didn't, either."

"Criminals do get off sometimes, you know."

Dallas poked at her salad while sorting through her jumbled thoughts. "We listened so carefully to everything." She glanced up at Amber. "Gabe's sister was very composed on the stand. You'd think someone who'd been through that would be more upset."

"How long had it been?"

"Four months."

"Did she have counseling in the meantime?"

"Yes, but—"

"That's what counseling does for you," Amber said. "It helps you deal with the trauma, so you won't get hysterical every time you think about what happened. I should know."

Dallas's eyes widened. "You?"

"I was raped when I was eighteen," she said evenly, as if giving a weather report.

"Oh, my God."

Amber's tone grew harsher. "Some guy I met at a party took me out in the desert. I was drunk, but he definitely raped me, the bastard." Her hand shook as she reached for her glass of iced tea and took a long, slow drink. The helpless fury remained in her eyes as she looked at Dallas. "I couldn't prove that, either, but my parents got me a good counselor, which is why I can talk about it now without breaking dishes."

Dallas reached across the table and covered Amber's hand with her own. "I wish I'd known. All this time we've been discussing this, you've probably been reliving what happened to you."

Amber sighed. "Some."

"I'm sorry." Dallas squeezed her hand.

"It's just that it's hard to prove, babe. You like your world to be all organized, and when it comes to this crime, everything's disorganized. This Celia and the rapist were the only people there. But I'll tell you this. If she says it was Neal Parnell, I'd believe her."

Dallas began to tremble. "You would? Even if the guy was wearing a ski mask and disguised his voice?"

Amber's laugh was short and humorless. "You can tell by the smell of his skin."

Goose bumps rose on Dallas's arms. "What?"

"You don't think you remember how a guy smells, do you? But the memory's there, all right. I'll bet if Gabe came up behind you, you'd recognize him without looking. You say Celia went out with this guy once, probably even kissed him. She'd remember the scent of his skin. Or at least a part of her mind would, even if she doesn't realize it. But of course something like that won't stand up in court."

"But the defense attorney said Celia was only trying to get back at Neal because he stopped taking her out. Celia doesn't have much money, and someone like Neal would be a good catch."

"So she accuses him of rape? What a great way to land a proposal."

"Of course not, but—" Dallas put down her fork and covered her face with her hands. "I'm so damned confused."

"Hey, it's not as if you did anything wrong," Amber said softly. "You had to go by the evidence."

Dallas combed her hair back from her face with trembling fingers. "If I helped turn a rapist back out on the streets, I *did* do something wrong. If only I could *know*."

"That's the tough part. But, Dallas, in the meantime, watch out for yourself, okay? Have Frank or Turner walk you to your car tonight. If you don't want Gabe around, that's your business, but in case he's right, protect yourself."

"I will." She sighed. "But it's the uncertainty that bothers me the most."

"You may have to live with that, babe."

BUT DALLAS KNEW that uncertainty was one thing she'd never been able to live with. She still had all the telephone numbers for her fellow jurors, and after a lackluster shopping spree with Amber she went home and called each one. She left several messages on answering machines, but was able to talk with three people. Each of them confirmed that they believed Neal was innocent.

"And he is innocent," Dallas told Gretchen as she locked her in the yard before driving off to work. "But in case I'm wrong, chew the hell out of anyone who comes around, okay?"

Gretchen wagged her tail and barked.

"Some killer dog you are." Dallas grinned and got into her truck. Then she scrambled back out, her heart hammering. On the seat of the truck lay a single red rose.

12

DALLAS WAS THROUGH her gate and back inside her locked trailer, Gretchen close by her side, inside of twenty seconds. Moments later she reemerged without Gretchen, her Lady Smith & Wesson cocked and ready in her hand.

She scanned the area around her trailer. Creosote bushes grew three or four feet high all over the desert floor. Any one of them could hide a grown man. In her imagination Neal crouched behind each one she studied.

A movement.

There! She aimed at the bush and fired, shattering the afternoon quiet. A huge jackrabbit bounded away unharmed, and she gasped in dismay. Trembling, she lowered the gun. She'd have to get hold of herself before she killed some innocent animal. Fighting panic, she worked her way through the gate, but she left it open for a quick retreat.

First she checked the back of the truck, but nothing was there except a few stray wisps of hay from Saturday. At last she opened the passenger side of the truck and looked in quickly, before spinning around to check behind her. A ground squirrel popped back in his hole, and Sugar and Spice moved restlessly in the corral, but otherwise the landscape remained the same.

After climbing into the truck, she sat beside the rose and locked both doors. Had she locked the truck after coming home from lunch with Amber? Probably not. She wasn't in the habit of doing that out here in the country. Obviously she'd have to start.

A note had been slipped under the stem of the rose. She could read it without moving the flower. Holding her breath, she scanned the brief message. *Sorry my dog got your dog in the family way. You're right. It's time for Igor to retire. Yours, George Stanhope.*

Dallas's laughter had an edge of hysteria to it. Was she going to live this way from now on, afraid of anything that suggested the presence of Neal Parnell? Would she panic every time she saw a black Corvette or red roses?

"No, by God," she said, getting out of the truck, the rose and note in one hand, her gun in the other. She went back into the house, looked up the number of the prosecuting attorney, Fred Axton, and dialed.

"Mr. Axton's in court right now," his assistant told her. "I'll be happy to take a message, Miss Wade."

"I need to speak with him as soon as possible. Do you think he could meet me at Rowdy Ranch sometime tonight? I'd be very grateful."

"I don't know, Miss Wade—" the assistant began.

"Please, it's very important," Dallas cut in.

"Well, I could certainly ask him."

"Thank you so much. Oh, and if he has any boots and jeans, this would be the time to wear them. Otherwise he'll stick out like a sore thumb."

"I'll tell him." The assistant sounded amused. "Will he have to do the Achy-Breaky?"

"I hope not."

The assistant laughed. "So do I. He's brilliant but uncoordinated. May I tell him what this is in reference to?"

"The sexual assault trial of Neal Parnell," Dallas said, taking a deep breath. "I want to know everything about it."

DALLAS WALKED QUICKLY into Rowdy Ranch, hating the unscheduled disturbance that had made her late. But she soon forgot about the time. Gabe stood by the pool table nearest her shop. He wore his black hat pulled low, so she couldn't see directly into his eyes, but she didn't need to see them to know his attention was focused like a laser on the front door.

His shoulders slumped in apparent relief when he saw her, and she wanted to cry. He'd been worried about her. Then he turned with that nonchalant movement of his hips she'd come to cherish and lined up his next shot as if he didn't care a hoot what happened to her. The rush of warmth she'd felt curdled in her stomach. She'd sent him away, and a man like Gabe didn't come knocking twice.

Cheeks warm, she walked past him without speaking, all the while remembering their grand entrance Saturday night. From the corner of her eye she assessed the reaction of the shop owners. Dave Fogarty was immersed in photographing a laughing group of four women attired in dance-hall costumes, but Irving Skinner, who ran the leather shop next to Fogarty's Fotography, seemed interested in Dallas's passage. Dallas also figured the animated conversation between Ted and Louise McNulty in the jewelry shop had something to do with her. After all, she and Gabe had put on quite a show on Saturday. For them to come in separately tonight and then not even speak to each other would provide the shop owners and staff at Rowdy Ranch enough gossip for the entire evening.

She unlocked the wrought-iron accordian gate that closed off her shop and pushed it back against the wall. A customer was already walking toward the shop. She felt Gabe's glance even with her back turned and wondered how she'd ever be able to concentrate on her work with him so close. She might have thought she'd severed the link between them, but a connection so powerful wasn't easily broken. With a sigh she turned on the lights and hung up her fringed jacket. She hoped Fred Axton took her message seriously and had some free time tonight. Otherwise it would be a very long evening.

ABOUT AN HOUR into her work schedule she realized she hadn't seen Neal yet. Then she looked for Beth and decided it might be Beth's night off. That could explain Neal's absence.

It also showed how ridiculous Gabe's claims were. Neal had simply become attracted to Dallas at the trial and been a little persistent in his pursuit, which was probably the way rich men operated. Now he'd moved on to Beth, and that would be the end of that. Dallas would find out from Fred Axton that all the evidence had been presented at the trial, and Gabe would have to face the fact that Neal was no threat, had never been one. Except Gabe would never admit that, and the issue would always stand between them, keeping them forever apart.

At a quarter to eight Fred Axton arrived while Dallas was finishing up a customer. She tried to hold back a smile when she saw him approaching the Cutting Pen. His jeans were cinched up too high at his waist, and beneath his rolled-up pant legs she glimpsed burgundy wing tips. He'd adorned his rugby shirt with a bola tie, and the high, rounded crown of his hat gave new meaning to the label "ten-gallon." Nobody would mistake Fred Axton for a cowboy.

He smiled when he saw her, and she decided it was safe to smile back. "Please sit down," she said, nodding toward one of the chairs lining one wall. "I'll be through in just a moment."

When her customer left, she sat next to Fred.

"How do I look?" he asked.

"Uh . . . different from how you looked at the trial."

"The outfit needs a little work." Fred stretched his legs out in front of him. "Bought these jeans about four years ago, never wore them. I think I might have picked up the wrong size." He shrugged. "I'll have them fixed before I come in here again."

"You've already decided to come back?"

Fred glanced out the door toward the dance floor, where people three rows deep were executing a line dance to "Boot-Scootin' Boogie." "Sure thing. I've been meaning to try this place for months." Dallas's reservations must have been obvious from her expression because he jumped to his own defense. "Hey, I watched 'Gunsmoke' when I was a kid. I can pick up on this."

He took off his hat and gazed at it. "Do you think this is too big?"

"It's not so much the size as the shape. Let me try something." Dallas took the hat over to the sink, turned the water on hot and held it over the steam while she reshaped the crown with a depression in the middle and a slant to the sides. Then she worked a curve into the brim so it didn't stick out like a Frisbee. "Try that," she said, returning the hat to him.

Fred stood and adjusted the hat in the mirror. "Not bad," he said. He swaggered up to the mirror. "You're dealing from the bottom of the deck, pardner." His chin jutted. "Oh, yeah?" He whipped two imaginary pistols from invisible holsters and fired them in quick succession. Then he blew smoke from the barrels, turned back to Dallas and flipped the phantom guns back into place.

Dallas laughed. During the trial, she had gotten the impression that he was a dynamic and intelligent man. Now she also saw that he had a playful side. "Old-fashioned justice."

"Sometimes I long for those days."

"I can see that, Mr. Axton."

"Fred. We go by first names out here in the West." He resumed his seat and shoved back his hat. "Now what do you want to know about the Parnell trial?"

"Whatever you can tell me." She felt a lump of nervousness rise in her throat.

He took off his hat and ran his fingers over the new crease in the crown. "I hated losing that one. But the plaintiff really loused up as far as helping us get a conviction. You did your job and I expected the verdict. We couldn't do ours."

Dallas tensed. "So you really think he was guilty?"

Fred looked at her for a long moment. "I don't just think. I know."

A movement by the bar suddenly drew Dallas's attention. Neal Parnell was there, dressed all in black.

GABE HADN'T PAID much attention to the guy in the rolled-up jeans when he'd entered Dallas's shop until Dallas sat down beside him and began an earnest conversation. The set of her shoulders told him this was no idle chitchat, so he'd left his beer on the counter of the bar and ambled over in that direction.

Then the guy took off his hat and a chill passed through Gabe. Fred Axton. Celia had pointed him out at the end of the trial, too. What in hell was Dallas doing talking to him? Had Gabe been missing the connection all along? Had she somehow influenced the case through the prosecutor?

He rejected the thought as unworthy even before it was fully formed. Love was blind, but not that blind. He wouldn't feel the way he did about Dallas if she had a rotten core. He had to believe that or doubt the entire meaning of his life.

No, she had some legitimate reason for talking to Axton, and the one that occurred to him built a small fire of hope in his heart. Maybe she had begun to doubt that Parnell was innocent, and she was gathering more information. He'd considered doing that himself, but had decided there was no point. He knew Parnell was guilty. But he could kick himself for not thinking to steer Dallas in that direction. Of course, she might not have done it if he'd made the suggestion.

He took a long, shaky breath. If she learned enough to shake her earlier convictions, would she come to him? He had to pray that she would.

HEART THUMPING, Dallas looked away from Neal. He wasn't facing her way, and she hoped to hell he hadn't recognized Fred. But Fred didn't look much like a prosecutor in his strange outfit. "I've had other people tell me they knew for certain Neal was guilty," Dallas said, gripping the edge of her chair seat. "But the evidence didn't support that. Was there something we didn't see?"

"Something you didn't hear."

Dallas held her breath.

"An enthusiastic detective set up an illegal wiretap, got a conversation between Parnell and one of his buddies when he bragged about 'getting the Martinez bitch.' The details fit her description of the events perfectly."

Dallas let out her breath and her blood pounded in her ears. "Oh, my God." She'd done it. She'd turned a rapist loose. She felt sick to her stomach.

"Hey, don't blame yourself. We couldn't use that evidence, and without it our hands were tied. But if he steps out of line again, believe me, we're going to nail his ass."

Fred's words of consolation had no meaning for her. Celia had been telling the truth, and she hadn't seen it. Instead she'd helped convince the jury not to convict Neal. She was responsible for a rapist walking free. Justice had not been done, and it was her fault.

She thought of telling Fred about her recent experiences with Neal, but something held her back. What had Gabe said? That he'd rather know where a rattlesnake was than scare it away and have to wonder where it would turn up next?

Heart hammering, she allowed her gaze to roam as much of the dance hall as she could see from her position inside the shop. Neal had disappeared. Then a man in black turned in profile and laughed before continuing a pinball game. Neal.

He slammed the side of the pinball machine, laughed again and walked toward the bar. Then, as if guided by some unholy sixth sense, he looked straight across the room toward her.

She got up casually and placed herself in front of Fred, blocking Neal's view of the man in her shop and Fred's potential view of Neal. "Well, what you've told me is all very interesting. But I guess it doesn't change the fact that Parnell is a free man."

Fred stood. "I'm afraid not. I thought of contacting you and other members of the jury after the trial and telling you what we knew, but I perceived you all as conscientious people who would beat yourselves up over this. Please don't. These things happen all the time."

"I won't beat myself up over it," Dallas lied, her tone grim.

"I hope not." Fred pulled his hat low over his eyes. Dallas noticed with satisfaction that he was much less recognizable with the brim curving a little over his face.

"Thanks for coming all the way out here tonight," Dallas said, offering her hand. If he left immediately, Neal might never know he'd been here.

"No problem. You know, as long as I'm out tonight, maybe I'll have a beer and try a few of those line dances."

Dallas fought panic. "Fred." She put her hand on his arm. She had to lean down a fraction to look into his eyes. "May I speak honestly?"

"Of course."

"In your profession I'm sure you've learned the importance of first impressions."

"Hmm." He glanced toward the dance floor.

"Many of the same people come back here night after night, Fred. They'll remember the rolled cuffs and the wing tips long after you've made the transition to tight jeans and Tony Lamas."

"I suppose you have a point." He touched the brim of his hat. "Thank you kindly, ma'am."

"Anytime."

His eyes twinkled. "Prepare yourself for the return of Fred Axton. It'll be a sight for sore eyes."

"I'm sure it will." With a sigh of relief she watched him leave the dance hall. From what she could tell, Neal didn't even notice the short man in the too-large jeans. But someone else had. Gabe stood, leaning slightly on his cue stick, and watched Fred until he pushed through the heavy oak doors into the night. Dallas turned away before Gabe could realize she was looking at him. She had some heavy thinking to do, and she wouldn't tip her hand until that thinking was done.

YEARS OF EXPERIENCE allowed Dallas to automatically shampoo and cut hair for the rest of the evening while she gave most of her attention to her problem. Near closing time she took a sealed envelope over to Dave Fogarty.

"Next time you have a chance, please give this to Gabe," she instructed.

Dave stroked his silvery beard. "Now, Dallas. This ain't junior high anymore."

"Don't I know it. I realize it looks juvenile, but I have my reasons why I don't want to approach him directly. Trust me, this isn't what you think."

"Okay, I'll do it. Mostly because I don't understand why you two split up all of a sudden, and I'd like to see you work it out."

Dallas had no idea if her plan would have any bearing on her relationship with Gabe. But like it or not, she needed his help. And she didn't want Neal to know she'd even asked for it.

At closing time she left without acknowledging Gabe at all. Pepper spray in hand, she unlocked her truck and climbed behind the wheel. She drove home, checking her rearview mirror constantly. No one she recognized followed her.

Once parked under her dusk-to-dawn light, she kept the pepper spray handy until she was safely inside her trailer with the door locked. Everything looked in order, but she toured the place, examining locks, checking closets and reassuring herself that she had her gun loaded and available in her bedside table drawer. Then she sat on her couch and waited, Gretchen at her feet.

To keep panic at bay, she focused on her plan, going over the details and testing it for flaws. She was sure there were some, but in general it was a good plan. The time dragged, and she clenched her cold hands in her lap and gazed at the pine paneling, imagining faces in the swirling knotholes.

A key clicked in the back door lock.

Hands clenched, she turned toward the sound as the door opened and Gabe stepped into her hallway. Her breathing quickened. He'd cooperated at least this much.

He approached her warily, the key in his hand. "If you gave me this, how did you get in?"

"I've always kept a key hidden out in the tack shed, under a saddle blanket."

"I wouldn't advise that anymore."

She held up the second key. "This is it. I won't put it back there again. Did you drive here through the wash?"

He nodded.

"Where's your truck?"

"I left it in the wash and hiked the rest of the way."

She grimaced. "That must have been a sacrifice. I know how cowboys hate to walk."

"I managed."

She shouldn't have expected anything but these taciturn responses, but they knifed through her, nonetheless. She waved him toward the rocker. "Have a seat."

"I'll stand."

"All right." She adopted his brusque attitude. "I'll make this quick. I have reason to believe that Neal Parnell did rape your sister, as you said."

His eyes flickered, but other than that he gave nothing away by his expression. She'd bet he was one hell of a poker player.

"Because I feel responsible for setting him free, I plan to help put him in jail, where he belongs."

Gabe hooked his thumbs in his belt loops and waited.

"I remember all the details from the trial, and my guess is he's more comfortable attacking someone in a deserted parking lot than breaking into their home, not that he wouldn't do that, if all else fails. But if I guide him to the parking lot, he'll try to rape me there, I think."

Gabe's stoicism vanished and his face contorted. "You'll *what?*"

Her heart hammered and breathing became difficult, but she continued. "I'm going to lure Neal into the parking lot. I'll spread some story around Rowdy Ranch that I'm staying late to do inventory." She chuckled without mirth. "It could be the truth. I am behind on that little chore, thanks to all that's happened."

His fists clenched at his sides. "Forget it."

She gazed into his dark eyes that burned with anger. "That's just it, Gabe. I can't forget it. I can't forget the trial, or Celia's testimony, or Neal's part in traumatizing her. I'm going to make it right by catching him in the act."

"No."

Her shoulders slumped. "I had hoped you'd help me. You and your two bounty-hunter friends."

He took a step forward. "If you think for one minute that I'd allow you to put yourself in—"

"Allow?" His use of the word propelled her from the sofa to brace herself in front of him. "How dare you imply you control me? You have nothing to say about it."

"The hell I don't." He grabbed her and hauled her against his chest. "I won't let you be the bait for that bastard."

The rich scent of him filled her nostrils. Amber was right. She'd know this man with her eyes closed. She longed to tangle her fingers in his hair, crush his lips to hers, but she struggled to put distance between them. As much as she wanted him, she wouldn't ever be dictated to.

He held her fast. "Listen to me, Dallas. Please."

"I'm doing this." She shoved hard at his chest. "With you or without you."

"You're crazy!" he gasped, holding her with effort. "Now be still and—"

"Never." She was panting, but she met his gaze straight on. "I'll never be still. I'll fight until the day I die to be my own person and make my own decisions. Got that, Escalante? Now let me go before I kick you in a very uncomfortable spot."

Slowly his arms came to his sides. He spoke through clenched teeth. "I've never met a woman like you."

She lifted her chin. "Then it's about time."

He continued to stare at her. When she stared back, he glanced away and rubbed the back of his neck. "You want to lure him into the parking lot?"

She sensed the tide might be changing in her favor. "Yes."

"Then what?"

"You'll be there. I checked tonight, and there's a Dumpster that would keep you hidden. I'll get him talking. You'll be the witness I need to show what his intentions are."

Gabe shook his head.

"What's wrong with that?"

"Everything. He might grab you before you get to me. He might somehow grab you inside the building."

"I thought of that. Station one of your friends inside. Neal doesn't know what they look like. You won't even be there that night, but your friend will. At closing time your friend can hide somewhere—inside a rest room stall or something—and be available if I need him. But I think Neal will try to get me outside, where he has a clear escape route."

He groaned. "You really think this is possible, don't you? You have no experience with criminals. You don't—"

"And what's the alternative? Do you enjoy hanging around this guy, waiting for him to make a false move? Do you want him to have that kind of power to keep your life on hold?"

"I won't put your safety on the line!"

"But I will," she said quietly. "And you're either in or you're out."

"If I say no, who would you get?"

She had no clue, but she didn't want him to know that. "I know some guys. I'm sure they'd help."

"Amateurs," he retorted.

She could feel him weakening. "Well?"

His sigh seemed torn from the depths of his chest. "Damn you, Dallas."

"Help me do this, Gabe."

His gaze was tortured. "I'd as soon be in hell."

"If you won't help me, that's where I'd wish you."

With a cry he turned away from her. After many long minutes he turned back, resignation and frustration obvious in the set line of his mouth. "I'd want both guys on this. One inside with you, another near the door where you'd come out, in case he grabs you there and tries to force you into his car or something."

"Fine, three of you, then. Four of us, counting me. We can do this, Gabe. We can hang this guy."

He stood, silent and brooding, in front of her. "How far am I supposed to let him go?" he asked quietly.

13

As Gabe waited for her answer, images assaulted him—of Parnell tearing at her clothes, of him putting his filthy hands on her skin and his insolent mouth on her lips. He closed his eyes as if to block out the ugly pictures. "How far, Dallas?"

"I . . . hadn't thought that out yet."

"I think you'd better consider that angle." He knew from the way her glance shifted that he'd hit a nerve.

Then her gaze swung back to him, the gray depths cold as slate. "Far enough that he thinks he's going to get away with it and starts saying things that will incriminate him." She lifted her chin. "I realize it will be . . . unpleasant, but I'll survive. When I think he's gone far enough, I'll shout a code word or something."

He felt the sharp pain originate in his heart and spread outward to his arms and fingers. The pain engulfed his stomach and plunged down his legs as his body rebelled at what she was saying. "And I'm supposed to watch him paw and insult you? What are you asking of me, Dallas?"

"I'm asking you to help me catch the man who raped your sister."

Something loosened in his chest, and the outpouring of anguish left him dazed. How he loved this woman! This stubborn, courageous, foolhardy woman. He stepped forward, his movements restrained, and touched her cheek. "All right," he said quietly.

She gazed up at him in wonder, then reached to brush her thumb across the corner of his eye. Only then did he realize his eyes were damp.

"You've asked me to willingly risk what is most precious to me," he said, his voice shaking. "Don't ever doubt the depth of that sacrifice." Then he swept her up in his arms, her warmth against his chest reassuring him, soothing his pain, as he carried her to the bedroom. He gazed into her eyes and saw mirrored there the same fierce agony that suffused him.

He closed the door, locking out the dog, and laid her on the bed. He undressed her slowly, carefully, as if she were a hologram that might dissolve if he moved too fast. With his own clothes he took less time, all the while holding her gaze with his.

When he finally lay next to her, she turned her face to him, like a flower moving toward the light.

"I love you," he murmured, brushing his knuckles across the pulse point at her throat. "But I didn't know until now how much. It seems I will do anything for you. Anything."

She didn't answer, and he was glad. A confession such as he had made required no answer. He'd humbled himself completely before her, and he hoped to God she would not take advantage of his vulnerability. The amount of trust he'd placed in her, through no conscious decision of his own, staggered him.

He leaned toward her, his hand cupping her cheek. "But now I need ... this ..."

Her lips parted in invitation.

"Dear Lord," he whispered, accepting the invitation.

He treasured everything—the sweet waft of breath as his mouth neared hers, the texture of her full lips, the supple movement of her tongue. With a touch light as a butterfly's wing he outlined the summit of each breast, the curve of her ribs, the dip of her waist to the swell of her hips. How smooth her thighs, how fragile the backs of her knees. He cherished her delicate ankles, which he circled with thumb and forefinger, and the graceful arch of each foot.

Ripples of awareness marked the passage of his touch, as a wheat field reveals the passage of the wind. She grew warm and trembly beneath his hand, and when at last he brushed across the cleft of her womanhood, he found her wet with desire.

He sheathed himself and moved over her, capturing her gaze as he slid slowly inside, gentle as a man initiating a virgin. He knew the wildness in her, knew she could match the wildness in him. But tonight there would be no ferocity in his touch, no desperation in his kiss. He moved unerringly forward until he rested securely within the cradle of her hips, her arms clasped around him. They paused, cocooned in each other, breath matching breath, heartbeat matching heartbeat.

His subtle rhythm was nearly imperceptible, yet she responded as he knew she would, from the depths that he touched with such soft insistence. Burgeoning desire rose within her, closing him securely inside her. He loved her the way driving rain penetrates rich dark earth, and she began to swell with promise. There was no sharp moment of release, only a deep thrumming that gathered speed until waves of passion washed endlessly through their locked bodies. When he could hold back no longer, his essence rushed forth in a torrent, joining with her, binding them together in silent testimony—a covenant forged between souls.

THEY DECIDED THAT GABE wouldn't appear inside Rowdy Ranch again and that no one should know of the plan except Gabe's two friends, Jasper and Diego.

That next evening during a break Dallas announced to Amber that the following night she'd stay late to take inventory.

Amber stopped repairing a nail she'd broken earlier. "Want me to stay and help?" Her offer lacked enthusiasm.

"No, thanks. You and Vince have plans. I can handle it."

Amber put down the emery board. "Wait a minute. I wasn't thinking straight. This isn't a good time for you to be here alone after closing. I am staying."

"Don't be silly. Neal Parnell hasn't bothered me in quite a while. See him out there having a good time with Beth?" The sight of Neal made Dallas's skin crawl, but she forced herself to seem nonchalant.

"I don't care. With Gabe out of the picture, I don't feel right about—"

"I won't be alone. Irving Skinner told me he's staying to take inventory, too." Dallas hated to lie to her friend, but Amber would throw up a million roadblocks if Dallas told her the truth.

"And you'll leave when Irving leaves?"

Dallas held up her hand. "I promise."

"Okay, then."

One down and one to go, Dallas thought, noticing that Neal had stopped at the bar for another beer. "I'm parched," she said. "Would you watch the shop while I get a soda from the bar?"

"Sure."

Dallas chose a spot halfway down the bar from where Neal sat. He didn't look at her. *What if he really has lost interest?* she thought, and was ashamed of the feeling of relief that surged through her at the possibility Neal wouldn't attack her, after all. But if she didn't send him to prison, he would rape someone else. She caught the attention of Tom, the bartender on duty.

"How's it going, Dallas?" he asked as he squirted soda from a nozzle into an ice-cube-filled glass.

"I'm so *behind,*" she said in a wail that she figured would carry down the length of the bar to Neal. "Looks like I'll have to stay after closing tomorrow night to take inventory."

Tom handed her the fizzing glass. "Bummer."

"Isn't it?" She started to turn away.

"Say, Dallas, what's the story on that guy, the one who always wears the flannel shirts? First you throw him out of your shop, then you act like you're going together, and now he's vanished."

He couldn't have fed her better lines if she'd handed him a script. "I should have followed my first instincts with that man, Tom. Let's just say it didn't work out. He's history."

Tom shook his head. "Dating's tough in the nineties, is all I have to say."

"No kidding." With a wave of her hand, Dallas returned to the shop with her drink. Unless Neal was hard-of-hearing, she'd just baited the trap.

WHEN SHE CAME HOME that night, Gabe was waiting. Their lovemaking was fervent and prolonged. They didn't speak of the next night's activities until early morning, just before Gabe returned to his truck hidden in the nearby wash.

"Forget this code-word business," Gabe said, holding her tight as they stood by her back door in semi-darkness. "I'll break things up when I think they've gone far enough."

"Don't step in too soon."

He didn't answer but his kiss was punishing, and he left without another word.

Dallas kept busy all day with chores. When she finally cleaned up and dressed for work late in the afternoon, her fingers shook as she fastened her bra and drew on her panties. Was she insane? Then she thought of Celia's testimony on the stand. At the time it had seemed too calm and rehearsed to be real. But it had been real. Celia had suffered through those things. And so would others, if Neal wasn't stopped now. She had a chance to stop him.

A light rain fell as she drove to work. Ordinarily she'd park near the door on nights like this, but instead she chose a spot near the Dumpster. Plenty of daylight remained as she got out of the truck and locked it. But it didn't take much imagination to picture the parking

lot as she knew it to be at night, with pockets of darkness beside parked vehicles and in corners where the
overhead lights didn't reach. She hurried toward the
building with the cowardly thought that maybe Neal
wouldn't come in tonight.

But he did. He'd dressed all in black again, and she
shivered as she contemplated why.

Diego had volunteered to be the inside man. Dallas
had never met him, but when he walked in she recognized him immediately from Gabe's description—
stocky, with a short dark beard and curly hair under a
battered western hat. Lacking the comfort of Gabe's
presence, Dallas kept her eye on Diego as a welcome
port in a stormy sea. She noticed that he drank only
soda during the evening.

"You okay?" Amber asked her about ten, when she'd
dropped a pair of scissors twice in five minutes.

"Too much coffee today," Dallas said. "I really have
to cut back on my caffeine."

"If you're nervous about staying here after closing,
I'll call Vince. We can all work on that damned inventory."

"I wouldn't dream of it." She'd tried to avoid looking at Neal tonight, but he always seemed to be hovering in her field of vision, although he'd never
acknowledged her. He moved like a panther through
the dance hall, making her constantly aware of his
menacing presence. She *was* jumpy, and if Amber had
picked up on her nervousness, Neal might. She'd have
to be more careful. "The inventory's no big deal," she
said.

"Well, I feel guilty, leaving you here, even if Irving Skinner is sticking around," Amber said.

"It's really no problem. I—my God."

"What?"

Dallas stared at the man sauntering toward her, a man with the power to ruin everything.

If circumstances had been different, he would have been, as he'd promised, a sight for sore eyes. A boldly patterned western shirt accentuated the breadth of his shoulders, and stone-washed jeans displayed well-muscled thighs and buttocks. Black lizard-skin boots added at least two inches to his height. His hat had been professionally blocked, and a tooled leather belt encircled his hips. Fred Axton had transformed himself into a cowboy.

Amber followed the direction of Dallas's gaze. "Cute, but too short for you. And falling for somebody on the rebound is *never* a good idea, Dallas. Put your eyes back in your head."

Dallas tried to gather her thoughts. "That's not why I'm staring. You should have seen him a couple of days ago. I'm amazed at the transformation." *And petrified that Neal will notice him and suspect something.*

"What'd he look like?"

"Not like that." Dallas couldn't see a way out of talking with Fred. He still didn't look much like the chief prosecutor for Pima County. Maybe she was worried for nothing. "You couldn't tell the guy had shoulders, or buns, either, for that matter."

"Well, you can now. Like I said, a couple of inches taller and I'd want to know his name."

"Well, I'll introduce you, anyway." Dallas smiled as Fred walked through the door of the shop. "I'm impressed," she said.

"I'm a quick study," Fred replied, his glance slipping toward Amber.

"Fred, this is my associate, Amber Dalton."

Fred extended his hand and gave Amber the direct gaze that Dallas had observed mesmerizing more than one female juror during the trial. Dallas watched with amusement as Fred's intensity brought a pleased flush to Amber's cheeks. Short or not, Fred might be about to give the unimaginative Vince a run for his money.

"Fred Axton was the prosecutor for the trial," Dallas continued as the handshake lasted a little longer than polite intercourse required.

"A lawyer, are you?" Amber asked.

"An urban cowboy," Fred responded. "Thanks to Dallas. She's my wardrobe consultant."

"She did a good job."

"Thanks." Fred took off his hat and tossed it on the rack. "But I think I need a finishing touch. How about trimming my hair, Amber?"

"Um, sure." Amber glanced at Dallas, who gave her a covert thumbs-up as Fred settled into the chair. Dallas had never been crazy about Vince, Amber's current boyfriend, and she couldn't think of a better matchup than Amber and Fred. They both were intelligent, principled people with a sense of humor. So what if Fred was an inch shorter than Amber? It wouldn't matter once they were prone.

Still, the niggling worry that Neal would recognize Fred plagued her. She searched the dance hall and found

Neal in a far corner, leaning with both arms braced against the wall, imprisoning a laughing Beth, who carried a tray of drinks. He seemed to have no interest in what was happening in the Cutting Pen. Rowdy Ranch was a huge place, after all. There were easily two hundred people within its confines tonight. No doubt she was imagining problems where there were none. Yet she'd be glad when Fred's hat was back on his head.

After receiving a very thorough shampoo and hairstyling from Amber, Fred walked over to the bar. Dallas didn't worry too much about it until she remembered Diego. She turned with a sense of foreboding, and sure enough, Fred had recognized Diego as a bail-enforcement officer.

Dallas watched helplessly as Diego made an excuse to get away from Fred, but it was too late. Dallas could tell the moment Neal recognized the prosecutor by the sudden stiffening of his posture and the abrupt end of his laughter. She turned away, heart racing, and tried to concentrate on the haircut she was giving. So what if Neal had recognized Fred? People from all over Tucson came to this place. But her plan no longer seemed so foolproof, and her palms grew slick with perspiration.

"I like your Fred Axton," Amber said after the customer left.

"Do you now?" Dallas seized the distraction like a lifeline. "Personally, I think he's a little short."

Amber threw a towel at her, and she ducked.

"Did you give him your number?" she asked.

"No. That wouldn't be fair to Vince."

"Oh." Dallas allowed her disappointment to show.

"But he gave me his."

"Oh! Good!"

Amber laughed. "Just in case. Don't get too excited. I told him I was going with someone."

"I see." Dallas smiled. "The conversation got that specific, then?"

"Let's face it. Vince has proposed about twenty times, and I always find some excuse to stall him. Should tell me something, shouldn't it?"

"I would say so."

Amber walked over to pick up the towel she'd thrown. "Funny how some people just click."

"Yeah."

Amber straightened, the towel in one hand, and looked directly at Dallas. "For example, I can't forget the picture of you and Gabe kissing over there by the pool tables. I don't care what you say. He's the right one. Maybe he went a little crazy when somebody raped his sister. What brother worth anything wouldn't? Cut him some slack." She peered at Dallas. "God, you have a peculiar look on your face. Are you sure you're okay?"

Dallas put a hand over her roiling stomach. She didn't need to talk about Celia's rape right now. "Must be something I ate."

"Go home after work, then. Forget the inventory."

"No." Dallas's voice sounded faint even to her own ears. She cleared her throat and spoke more forcefully. "I'll feel better when it's done."

"Did anyone ever tell you that you're stubborn?"

"Yes," Dallas said, and glanced for the hundredth time at the clock.

GABE WISHED that he smoked. He needed something to pass the time as he and Jasper sat in his truck parked a block from Rowdy Ranch. Jasper wasn't much of a conversationalist. As they sat silently in the chilled cab, Gabe fooled with his watchband, snapping it repeatedly.

"Damn, but you're making me nervous," Jasper said. "And I don't get nervous."

Gabe stopped snapping the band. "Sorry." Jasper's calm temperament was one of his most endearing characteristics. An ex-wrestler, he had the kind of body that required custom clothes. When people saw Jasper, they instinctively drew back, until he smiled his gap-toothed smile and gave them a cheerful greeting.

Jasper liked everybody, unless he learned they'd run afoul of the law. Then he perceived it as his mission to bring them to justice. He accomplished this without rancor, but his brutal efficiency was legendary among bounty hunters. Gabe hadn't sent him inside Rowdy Ranch because he might have been recognized. And even if he hadn't, Jasper never went unnoticed for long.

"We should be able to take our positions in about fifteen minutes," Gabe said. "Remember, if he comes out with her, don't even take time for the radio. Just get him, as long as you can do it without Dallas being hurt."

"Right. And if he comes out alone, I'll follow him and

hide next to the electrical box." Jasper hit his fist into the palm of his hand. "We're gonna nail this sleazoid."

"Yeah." Gabe decided he couldn't sit there any longer. He opened his door and glanced over at Jasper. "I think we're close enough to the time. Ready?"

Jasper nodded.

"Then let's go."

14

VINCE ARRIVED to pick up Amber as Rowdy Ranch began to empty out. Fortunately Irving Skinner hadn't left, which gave support to Dallas's story that Irving was also staying late to take inventory.

While Amber finished cleaning up her station, Vince held Dallas captive with a long-winded story about his latest softball triumph. When Amber left with Vince, she glanced over her shoulder and rolled her eyes. Dallas smiled, figuring she might not have to listen to many more of Vince's stories. Even if Fred told stories, they'd at least be more interesting than anything Vince could dish out.

One by one the shop owners pulled the black accordion doors across the front of their shops.

"Inventory, huh?" Shirley Jorgenson from the T-shirt shop commented as she walked by on her way out the door.

"Afraid so," Dallas said, looking official with a clipboard in one hand.

"Got mine done last week, thank God."

"Lucky you." Dallas watched Shirley walk out the door accompanied by Frank, one of the bouncers. Shirley didn't like mace or pepper spray, claiming they always detonated in the heat that built up in the interior of her car on warm Arizona days. So she opted for an escort. *Something's terribly wrong when women can't walk alone at night without fear,* Dallas thought. She took a deep breath. Tonight she'd do her part to combat the terrorism that had become the norm.

Only a few dancers remained on the floor. Diego had left his position by the bar, but Dallas had expected that. According to the plan, Diego would now be standing on a toilet seat in the men's rest room, crouched low so no one could detect his presence. Dallas hadn't seen Neal recently, either, although Beth was still around. Was Neal in the parking lot, deep in the shadows, waiting? Fear tightened in her chest and quickened her heartbeat. She swallowed and took several deep breaths.

Eventually the deejay played the final song of the night, and the last few stragglers left. The gel lights and neon were extinguished in favor of clear overhead lights that dispelled much of the magic that drew Rowdy Ranch customers. In the overhead glare Dallas noticed worn spots on the dance floor and stains on the carpet. The sound of vacuum cleaners replaced the seductive country-western music, and the wait staff scurried back and forth with clean glassware and fresh stacks of napkins.

At last one of the managers wandered over to Dallas's shop. "We're ready to take off," he said. "You know which door to use when you go out."

"Right." The double doors in front and the delivery doors on the side were fitted with security bolts and the managers had the only key. Dallas could go out a back door, which would automatically lock behind her.

"Just throw on the alarm system when you leave," the manager said.

"Sure thing." Cool sweat trickled down her backbone. "See you tomorrow night." Tomorrow night seemed aeons away, a safe time when everything would be over. She wanted it to be tomorrow night . . . now. The manager and the last of the wait staff walked out the back door.

She was alone. Except for Diego. Maybe she should go find him and tell him the coast was clear.

She walked toward the rest rooms, where one door depicted a pendulous cow and the other picture, pendulous in a different fashion, depicted a bull. She'd always resented those pictures, she thought as she headed toward the bull. Men might preen at being compared to a well-hung bull, but no woman she knew appreciated being compared to a cow.

As she lifted her hand to push open the door, the dance hall was plunged into darkness.

She whirled, her heart racing. Had there been a power failure? What a damned rotten time for it!

But there had been no power failure. A single slash of purple neon flickered on, bathing the hall in a dim, otherworldly glow. Dallas strained to pick out a movement in the deep shadows but could see no one.

Then the sound system began to play, and George Strait's voice filled the hall. Dallas's mouth went dry and she stopped breathing. The song was "When Did You Stop Loving Me?"

"Diego!" she screamed, pushing open the door.

"Forget Diego," said a microphone-assisted voice over the music.

With a strangled sob, she dashed for the only door that would open, but a black figure, crouched and ready to spring, blocked her escape. "Just try it," he whispered. "I like it when they fight."

She backed away from him and tried to unfreeze her brain. She had to figure this out. Had to be smarter than he was. She quickly calculated her position. To her left were the rest rooms, to the right the dance floor. Directly behind her, maybe ten yards away, was one of the bars.

If she talked, she might distract him enough to take defensive action. "You knew," she choked out.

"That you'd stopped loving me?" he drawled, mimicking the song. "I've suspected for a while." He moved toward her as she inched away. He seemed in no hurry. "The idea of a trap crossed my mind when you so conveniently announced you'd stay late. But seeing that bastard Axton was the final clue. I'd been trying to place the guy with a beard, and when Axton talked to him I remembered the face. Saw him a couple of times the past few days, thought it was coincidence. But it wasn't coincidence, was it, Dallas? Your boyfriend hired him to follow me, didn't he?"

As the George Strait number ended, her hands closed on the back of a chair. Using the same motion as roping a calf, she hurled the chair at him.

He dodged the chair and laughed as it thudded harmlessly on the carpet behind him. "I knew this would be fun."

A new song began, a more suggestive one. *Let's get together for that old bump and grind*, sang a new country star.

"Diego!" Dallas screamed again as she eased toward the bar.

You're just the sort of girl to make me lose my mind.

Neal stalked her, the left side of his face outlined in violet, the right thrown into shadow. The silver buttons on his black shirt gleamed dully in the ghostly light. His dark western hat shaded his eyes, those pale eyes she'd once thought babyish. "Your bearded friend won't be coming," he said.

She stared at the movement of his full lips, heavy with carnality. Her stomach heaved. "You killed him."

"No. I'm not a killer, Dallas. Sweet Dallas. Haughty Dallas."

"Then where is he?"

"Passed out in the bathroom." His teeth gleamed carnivorous and sharp in the neon glow. "Lucky for me I keep a few drugs in the car. Never know when they'll come in handy. When I told Beth the guy would be laying for me tonight, she agreed to slip something into his drink. You see, Beth will do about anything for me."

And so, sweet darlin', if you're inclined to be kind...

Dallas felt the padded edge of the bar against her back. "If she knew what you are, she wouldn't."

We'll get together for that old bump and grind.

Neal sneered and stepped closer. "It was that puny little prosecutor who turned you around, wasn't it? You used to like me. I know you did. But he told you I was guilty, and you believed that runt instead of me."

"You raped Celia, didn't you?"

Bump, bump, bump and grind.

"Such an ugly word, rape." His voice reminded her of oil dripping. "What happened between Celia and me wasn't like that at all. She liked it. She told me so."

"Because you threatened to kill her if she didn't say what you wanted?" Praying that the shadows hid her movements, she slipped one hand behind her, groping until her fingers closed around the neck of a bottle.

"Ah, Dallas, we say lots of things in the throes of passion, don't we? I'm sure you've said violent things to that stud of yours—what's his name? Gabe?"

She'd have to smash the bottle against the counter hard enough to break it. Then, with luck, she'd have a weapon. "Never mind what his name is."

"Is he waiting outside the building? I found a radio on his bearded friend."

Dallas had a moment of hope. If the radio was still in the bathroom, she might be able to reach it.

"I had to smash the radio," he said, as if reading her thoughts. "Although I doubt your hero could get in here, anyway. The bolted doors would be impossible, and the back door locks from the inside unless you have a key. I don't suppose he has one?"

Come on, baby, it's time to lose our minds.

She clenched her teeth together. Gabe had no key. The managers had jealously guarded the possession of keys after several cases of liquor had been stolen one night. "I gave him a key," she said.

"I don't think so. Beth explained to me about the key situation when I mentioned it might be fun to sneak in here and have sex in the middle of the dance floor. She liked the fantasy. We couldn't decide whether to do it in neon light or the revolving ball. I think I prefer the

neon, don't you?" He glanced once toward the purple
slash on the opposite wall.

She grabbed the brief moment to whip the bottle out
and crack it against the counter. Bourbon splashed over
her. The sudden stench of alcohol made her gag, but the
bottle neck held together. She pointed the jagged glass
at him.

"Oh, my." He reached down, keeping his gaze on her,
and pulled something from his boot. When he crouched
lower and began circling toward her, the violet light
flickered across a long blade. "Ever had experience in
knife fighting, sweet thing?"

A new song came on the sound system. Hysterical
laughter bubbled in Dallas's throat as she imitated
Neal's stance. *And I'm going crazy, no matter how cool
I seem*, crooned the familiar song. She'd never been in
a knife fight in her life. But if she expected to disable
him, she had to get close enough to cut him with the
bottle.

'Cause she is the answer to this cowboy's dream.

She watched his knife hand weave a pattern in the air,
and she gripped the neck of the bottle as he closed in.
She would aim for the stomach in one long motion,
follow through like sending a cue stick into the white
ball. One lunge and back out, away from that weaving
knife. The music created an eerie tempo as he maneuvered closer, almost stepping in time.

"Care to dance?" he whispered.

With a yell she leaped forward. He caught her wrist
when it was only halfway to its target. His fingers bit
into her flesh. His face came within inches of hers. He
raised the knife.

GABE SCANNED the damp parking lot again. The rain had stopped, leaving the asphalt slick and shining in the overhead mercury lights. Nearby creosote bushes gave off the acrid scent of the desert after a rain. Nothing moved. He was almost sure Parnell wasn't out there. He flicked on the radio and spoke softly to Jasper. "No sign of him?"

"Nothin', Gabe. Either the guy left early or—"

"I don't like it. I'm signaling Diego."

"Just a minute, Gabe. I know you're antsy, but I'm not sure everybody else is outta there. If some manager's still around and a radio goes off . . . Diego would have a tough time explaining why he was hiding in the men's rest room."

Gabe had to trust his gut. "Then we'll go in and help him explain. I'm calling him." He punched in the code and waited. When nothing happened, he felt as if somebody had threaded an ice pick up his spine. He punched the number again. Then he punched in Jasper's code. "He's not answering."

"Maybe he's—"

"We're going in."

"How are we going in? I may be strong, Gabe, but I can't break through any of those doors, and neither can you."

"Stay there. I'm getting the truck." He cut Jasper off in the middle of his startled oath of surprise and sprinted down a back alley, slipping twice mud but regaining his balance each time. Along the way he tossed the radio in the bushes. The damn thing was no good. No good!

Wrenching open the door he leaped into the truck, the key already positioned for the ignition. He cranked once and the engine stayed silent, as if knowing the sacrifice he was about to ask. Cold sweat bathed his armpits. He cranked again, and the engine started. Throwing the truck into gear, he roared down the street. He thought of all the times he'd pushed open the oak doors that led into Rowdy Ranch. Thick suckers. Driving one-handed, he fastened his seat belt.

"DROP THE BOTTLE, sweet thing."

Dallas watched in horrified fascination as the knife blade descended slowly toward her throat.

"Drop it." He squeezed harder, cutting off the circulation to her fingers.

She felt the bottle slipping from her grasp, tried to keep her grip and failed.

'Cause she is the answer to this cowboy's dream.

The bottle shattered on the floor.

"Good girl. I don't want to cut you. You'll be so much more fun alive than dead."

The reminder of his ultimate intention snapped her from her hypnotized state. Putting all her weight into it, she whacked her knee into his crotch.

An ugly expletive wheezed out of him as he released her and doubled over. Her shop was closer than the door to the outside. She could lock herself in. And there were scissors, and solutions to throw in his face. She ran across the polished dance floor as the finale to "A Cowboy's Dream" crescendoed around her. She'd nearly reached the other side of the floor when he tackled her from behind. She went down and felt a sharp pain ram from her wrist up the length of her arm.

"That wasn't nice," he panted, rolling her over as she struggled to regain her wind. His hat was gone, his eyes wild, his hair disheveled and backlit in purple.

This was the Neal that Celia Martinez had seen, she thought. If the jury had seen the transformation in Neal's baby face, even for a brief moment, they would never have acquitted him.

"Now it'll only go worse for you," he rasped.

The music changed again. This time, she recognized the song she'd waltzed to with Gabe. Neal must have watched them constantly, and the memory of that song had been burned into his fevered brain.

She fought him, despite the excruciating pain in her wrist. She scored one scratch to his cheek as he struggled to get her blouse open. He no longer had the knife, but he was strong, far stronger than she. His breath reeked of beer and he stank of sick desire. The more she struggled, the brighter grew the light in his eyes.

"Is this what you need to get excited?" she taunted, trying to kick him as he pinned her legs with one thigh. "I'll bet you don't even know what normal sex is."

The waltz soared through the empty hall as if seeking out dancers.

"Shut up." He held her wrists so tight she bit her lip to keep from crying out at the pain. He wanted her cries, and she wouldn't give them.

"I'll bet you can't even do it with Beth, can you?" she choked out. "You're impotent with her, aren't you?"

"Shut up, bitch!" He tightened his hold on her.

Mute with the pain from her bad wrist, she stared at him through swimming eyes.

"That's more like it. Now I'll kiss you and make everything better."

When his revolting lips descended toward hers, she spat in his face.

He looked up, her spit running down one cheek. She had never seen anyone look like that. His pupils seemed to be twin black holes leading to a bottomless pit, or the depths of hell. He circled her throat with one hand, his thumb pressing against her windpipe. Slowly, his jaw clenching with the effort, he squeezed. She tried to free herself, but she was weakening. The room began to spin and grow darker. The waltz faded slowly away. A rumbling noise sounded in the distance, or was it her own blood churning through her veins?

There was an explosion. Perhaps death came like that, a rending and tearing from this physical world. She would have imagined death would be quieter. Then she blacked out.

THE IMPACT JAMMED the engine block back, but not far enough to crush Gabe's legs. The seat belt held, but his arms felt as if he'd been operating a jackhammer. Through a fog of steam coming from his ruptured radiator, the doors to Rowdy Ranch looked like bomb damage he'd seen in the Middle East. But there was an opening big enough to fit through. And although it didn't make sense, he could hear music.

He fumbled for the door latch, which seemed to be missing. Finally he put his shoulder to the door and shoved until it gave. When he leaped out, Jasper was standing there like a stone monument to perpetual amazement, his mouth open, his eyes wide.

"We're in," Gabe said, and headed for the opening.

Jagged pieces of wood ripped at his clothes and scratched his skin as he shoved his body through the opening, but he didn't feel any pain. Once inside, he had to take a moment to adjust his eyes to the weird purple light. Then he saw her, lying across the edge of the dance floor. He felt dizzy.

"There he goes!" Jasper shouted, and sprinted after a figure in black heading toward the back door.

Gabe barely paid them any attention. He walked unsteadily toward the crumpled woman and dropped to one knee beside her. "Dallas?" He forced himself to put his hand to the side of her neck. When her pulse beat softly against his fingers, he wept and gathered her into his arms.

Slowly she roused as his hot tears fell on her face. "Gabe?"

He couldn't speak. With trembling hands he smoothed her hair back from her face.

"Did you get him?" she whispered.

"I don't know."

She frowned. "Where is he?" Her voice was raspy and bruises were appearing on her throat. He must have tried to choke her.

"I don't know."

"You have to get him."

"I—"

"Or all this is for nothing." She grabbed his shirt in surprisingly strong fingers. "Gabe!"

She was right. Slowly he lowered her to the floor again and stood. Over by the exit door he could hear the fight. He started in that direction, to help Jasper.

Except Parnell must have wriggled free of Jasper, because a figure dressed in black was suddenly coming at Gabe, obviously headed for the opening in the oak doors. But he couldn't get there without passing by Dallas. And Gabe could never let him get near Dallas again. An unhuman cry rose to his lips as he launched himself at Parnell.

The man would be easy to kill, he thought as his knuckles connected with Parnell's gut and the air whooshed out of him. Parnell went down and Gabe dragged him back up, planning to finish the job. It would be easy to do.

"Gabe, no!"

Her voice reached him from a great distance. Hadn't she just told him to get Parnell? Hadn't she given him permission to wipe him from the face of the earth? With the next blow, Parnell's jaw gave way with a satisfying crunch and he went down like a rag doll.

"Gabe, don't become an animal! Please God, don't become like him."

She was crying now. He paused to listen, confused.

Jasper came up and gazed down at Parnell. "I'd kill him. Don't give another jury a chance to let him off," he said in a perfectly even tone of voice. "Self-defense. I'm your witness."

Gabe turned back toward Dallas, and the red haze of his blood lust drifted slowly away. With uncompromising clarity he took in the look of horror on her face, a look that told him all he needed to know. She'd seen the savage in him, seen it reflected in one of his closest friends. Then he glanced at Jasper. "Better call the police," he said.

"Think about your sister, man," Jasper pleaded. "You know the deal. The guy's got money. He'll appeal for years. He'll get paroled. He'll probably study law in prison, if he even goes there, and find a way to sue for mistreatment."

Gabe sighed. "Call the police, Jasper. And the paramedics, while you're at it."

15

"SO, DALLAS, what's your current thinking about Gabe?" Amber asked. "Do you miss him?"

Mounted on Sugar, Dallas rode ahead of Amber and Spice through a quiet canyon in the Tucson Mountains. It was the first week in April, a month after the nightmarish incident at Rowdy Ranch, and March rains had scattered purple lupine and gold daisies over the desert floor.

"I thought we'd agreed not to bring up the subject of Gabe," Dallas said.

"You agreed. I didn't."

Dallas sighed. "Gabe is a leaving kind of man," Dallas said. "End of discussion."

"I don't believe that. Something more is going on."

"I'll tell you what's going on." Dallas guided Sugar around an outcropping of granite. "I ceased to be interesting once he caught the bad guy. Now he's off in Bolivia, getting his kicks chasing another criminal. I was important for the run of the show. Now the show's over."

"I don't believe that." Amber shifted in her saddle and Spice blew air through his nostrils. "And neither does your horse."

"Then why didn't Gabe say anything before he left? Why didn't he tell me to wait for him, and all that garbage men always say, even if they don't mean it? He didn't even have the decency to pretend he was coming back!" Sugar's ears flicked nervously at Dallas's angry tone. "Sorry, girl." Dallas patted the silky neck, although her touch was awkward. She'd be glad when the cast could come off her wrist in a couple of weeks.

"Well, Fred's been talking to Jasper and Diego, and they all think—"

Dallas groaned. "Look, I like Fred. You know I do. I'm happy you two are going out. But no way could someone like Fred understand Gabe Escalante."

"Okay, have it your way. Gabe's a creep who used you for his own ends, and there's no reason you two should see each other again. Even if Gabe is due back in town today, and even if Fred did offer to invite him to Rowdy Ranch, you wouldn't want to see him, so I'll tell Fred to forget it."

Dallas felt as if someone had just punched her in the stomach. "Fred . . . Fred was going to invite him to Rowdy Ranch tonight?"

"Yeah, but I can see it's no use. Both Jasper and Diego thought he'd go, too. They have some theory that Gabe thinks you don't want him around because he's such a violent guy."

Dallas pulled Sugar to a halt and turned in her saddle. "What did you say?"

Amber smiled. "Finally I have your attention. Let's get down and set a spell, as they say."

Dallas's legs were shaky as she dismounted. Leading Sugar, she headed for a smooth, sunny rock that would seat two. She was careful not to step on any wildflowers as she walked to the rock and sat, holding Sugar's reins loosely in one hand.

"Ah, nothing like something to warm your buns," Amber said, levering herself down beside her. Both horses began munching sprigs of tender young foxtail grass.

The relaxing warmth of the April day did nothing to calm Dallas's turbulent stomach. "Okay, Amber. What's been going on?"

"Well, Fred and I naturally talk about you. You've been so depressed and everything."

"I have not!"

"See? You're so depressed you don't even know you're acting depressed."

"That's bull."

"Think what you think. Your friends are worried about you. Dave Fogarty considered taking up a collection among the shop owners to send you on a cruise or something."

Dallas stared at her. "You're kidding."

"Nope."

Dallas moved her finger over the signatures decorating her cast, and a lump formed in her throat. "They're good people."

"Good, but not too perceptive. They all thought Gabe was a dead issue. I didn't. So I pestered Fred to interrogate those two friends of Gabe's."

"Interrogate?" She glanced up. "Good Lord, Amber."

Amber shrugged. "I'm picking up some of the lingo. Sorry. I meant he asked some questions. And the answers describe a guy who's sure he's too rough around the edges for you. He thinks you see him as a savage who enjoys beating people up."

Dallas felt light-headed. "Amber, he *saved my life*. How could I possibly judge his actions? He did what he thought was necessary. And he didn't kill Neal, when I know every instinct told him to do it. Even Jasper told him to."

Amber looked at her. "Yeah, well, you know how these guys jump to conclusions, and they can't communicate worth a damn. He already had it in his head that he wasn't the man you wanted. And once upon a time you told me the same thing."

Dallas's heart thudded painfully. Surely Gabe couldn't think that she'd reject him. Not after all they'd shared. "I didn't really know him when I said that. And I was afraid he'd be like my father and stepfather, always trying to run things. I didn't know the difference between a bully and someone with inner strength."

"But you didn't tell him any of that stuff later on."

"I should have." Dallas twisted the reins in her hand. "But there was the business with Neal and . . ."

"And some wonderful times in bed," Amber finished for her. "That can distract a woman from conversation real easy."

Dallas's face warmed. "But I still can't believe he thinks I have a low opinion of him."

"It seems he remembers you referring to 'reckless bounty-hunter mentality.' I can certainly believe you said that, Dallas."

Guilt washed over her. "But that was before I—" *Before I fell in love*, she finished silently.

"Also, Jasper said Gabe's first wife left him because she hated his job. So Jasper figured out—and mind you, Gabe didn't explain this to him—Jasper figured out that on that horrible night, when you were screaming at him not to become an animal, he decided he'd better get out of your life for good."

"Oh, God." Dallas buried her face in her hands and fought tears.

Amber put an arm around her shoulders. "But I guess that's not what you wanted, was it, sweetie?"

Dallas shook her head.

"I had to make sure before I gave Fred the go-ahead. You see, Gabe's two buddies are very protective."

"I know," Dallas murmured, head down. "Once Jasper and Gabe were sure I was okay, they tore back to the rest room to find Diego." She shuddered. "Thank God he only ended up with a massive headache and a wounded ego. Neal could have killed him."

"And if he had, he'd be dead now himself."

Dallas stared at the pebbled ground. "I wouldn't have blamed them for doing that."

"Good. Then you'll understand that if Diego and Jasper thought for a moment you'd give Gabe the boot tonight, they'd move heaven and Earth to keep him away from you."

Dallas lifted her head and swiped at her eyes. "I won't give him the boot, Amber."

"You're sure? What about that fabled need to be in control, to be independent?" Amber gazed at her and waited.

Dallas thought of the past few weeks without Gabe. Oh, she'd been able to come and go as she pleased without considering another person. She'd made all her own decisions. None of them had seemed worth making without Gabe there. "Gabe once predicted that we'd fight a lot if we stayed together, but he said it would keep life exciting."

Amber's eyes sparkled with understanding. "It's great to meet your match, in every sense of the word."

Dallas nodded. "Maybe his unpredictable traveling and the constant danger will bother me. Maybe my compulsive neatness and stubborn streak will bother him. But I...love him so much I was willing to take the risk. When he left I decided he wasn't."

Amber touched her hand. "You owe it to yourself to find out."

"How will I know if he's coming or not?"

"Not until they walk in, I'm afraid. Fred's in court all day today, and he told me to leave a message with his assistant if I wanted him to call Gabe. And then there's always the chance they won't link up. Fred said he'd come in tonight, whether he brings Gabe or not, but he probably won't know what's happening until the last minute." She patted Dallas's knee. "Sorry to put you through that."

Dallas gave her a watery smile. "Beggars can't be choosers."

IT WAS A TYPICAL TGIF crowd, boisterous and ready to party. Business at the Cutting Pen was brisk, for which Dallas was thankful.

"I think I'm more nervous than you are," Amber said, glancing at the doors each time they opened. They were no longer made of solid oak. An oak veneer, not as intricately carved as the original doors, covered a metal core that the managers swore a tank couldn't penetrate.

The Rowdy Ranch slogan had been repainted over the door, and Dallas had taught herself not to look at the slash of purple neon that had illuminated the deeds of that awful night. Beth had been arrested and would no longer work at Rowdy Ranch. The blood stains had been cleaned from the carpet.

Best of all, Dallas didn't have to fear Neal Parnell might come into the dance complex. The judge, knowing the nearly unlimited resources of the Parnell family, had ordered him held without bail in the Pima County jail until the trial. Celia had called Dallas to thank her, but Dallas had declined Celia's lunch invitation. Talking with Celia would only remind Dallas that Gabe was lost to her.

"What are you going to do when he comes in?" Amber asked during a lull between customers.

"*If* he comes in."

"Okay, *if*. But I'm betting he will."

Dallas glanced at her in horror. "Don't tell me people are placing bets on this!"

Amber laughed. "Actually, Dave suggested it and I told him you'd never forgive us."

"That's for sure. So I assume you told everybody that Gabe might show up tonight?"

"Well, yes, I did. They've been suffering through this with you, you know. Shirley Jorgenson said you've ignored her several times, and Ted and Louise McNulty said you've been very short with them, too."

"I didn't mean to be, Amber. I'll make it up to them. We'll have a big barbecue at my place sometime soon."

"If you think it's definitely called for. Irving Skinner still hasn't gotten over being the decoy when you pretended you and he were taking inventory together."

Dallas gazed at her. "You're still upset about that, too, aren't you?"

"Yes," Amber said quietly. "I thought we were friends."

"We are, which is why I didn't tell you. You would have tried to stop me."

"Of course I would have tried to stop you, you idiot! That was the dumbest stunt I've ever heard of."

"But Neal's in jail now."

"And you could be dead. Not a good trade, in my opinion."

"I did what I thought I had to."

Amber shook her head. "You and Gabe certainly deserve each other. If it's possible to breed this excessive nobility into your genes, the two of you will give birth to the next Nathan Hale or Joan of Arc."

The idea of having Gabe's children struck Dallas dumb.

"Ha," Amber said. "Gotcha again. You have a real case on the guy. So what are you going to do when he comes in? Let's think of something dramatic."

"Let's not."

"Come on, Dallas. Your friends deserve a tear-jerking wrap-up to this story. How about asking him to dance? I can give the deejay a signal, and he can play something special. What'll it be?"

Dallas swallowed the lump in her throat. "A waltz."

"Great choice. Any particular waltz?"

Dallas didn't think she could bear to dance to the waltz Neal had sullied with his sick behavior. "No, I guess not."

"Then I'll make a suggestion. That wonderful old Anne Murray number, where she asks the guy if she can have this dance for the rest of her life. That would be perfect. You wouldn't have to say a word."

Dallas took a shaky breath. "He probably won't come."

"I'm going to set it up with the deejay, anyway. Can't hurt. Can you take this next customer while I run over there?"

Before Dallas could protest, Amber left. Dallas seated the man and reached for the massage wand. It was getting late. She didn't know how much longer she could stand the waiting.

As she was shampooing the customer, Amber walked back in, looking worried.

Despite the fact they seldom discussed personal business in front of customers, Amber walked over to the shampoo bowl. "Fred just arrived," she said.

Dallas's stomach began to churn.

"I'm sorry, Dallas. He's alone."

She clutched the edge of the shampoo bowl for support.

"But he left a message on Gabe's machine. He could still come in, you know. He's probably been delayed, or he has a lot to do or—"

"Or he doesn't want to see me," Dallas said through an aching haze that threatened to overwhelm her.

"I'll finish this," Amber said, motioning her away from the customer. "Take a break. And don't give up."

But she had. She couldn't ride this roller coaster any longer. She remembered what it had felt like a month ago, when she'd been involved with Gabe. The uncertainty of the relationship was the part she'd hated, even as she'd loved the excitement. She couldn't keep herself dangling like this. With Gabe, it might be a pattern, and it was a pattern she couldn't live with.

In the rest room she dabbed at her eyes and took several long, calming breaths. The hell with him. She'd had a life before Gabe, and she'd have one again. She had her business and her place in the country. Once Gretchen gave birth to her mongrel puppies, Dallas could get back to her plans of breeding purebreds.

She walked out of the rest room, and straight into Gabe's arms.

He caught her and held her slightly away from him so he could look into her eyes. She stared back, drinking in the sight of him while her heart chugged like a freight train going up a steep rise. He wore no hat, and in the light pooled near the rest room area he looked haggard, with dark smudges under his eyes. His dark gaze searched hers. Then he reached down and brought her injured wrist, cast and all, to his lips.

The remembered scent of him drew her closer. She touched his hair, grown shaggy around the collar of his flannel shirt. A Doug Stone song ended, and Dallas held her breath. When Anne Murray's full-throated voice filled the dance hall, she felt dizzy, but kept her balance by looking into Gabe's eyes.

Her voice trembled. "Would you . . . like to dance?"

"I would like that very much." He cupped her elbow and guided her to the floor. When they reached the polished boards, she turned and held out her arms. He swept her up, making her forget the bulk of the cast on her wrist, the agony of weeks without him, the pain of his imagined desertion. The sweet warmth of his embrace brought tears to her eyes.

They whirled around the floor, and she saw only him in the spinning colored lights. His hands were sure, his step unerring, his gaze locked with hers.

"You got Fred's message," she murmured.

"Yes."

"What did he say?"

His voice was husky. "That you wanted me. But I wasn't sure what—"

"Listen," she said.

And as the words of Anne Murray's song surrounded them, the haggard lines slowly left his face, and the dark warrior eyes softened and began to glow with love. Vaguely Dallas realized that no other dancers were on the floor. Then, from the crowd surrounding the dance floor, came a smattering of applause. The applause soon swelled to a roar as shouts and cheers filled Rowdy Ranch.

Epilogue

Five months later

"I'm home," Gabe called, opening the front door into the trailer. Then he realized his mistake as the floor shook under the galloping paws of the army coming down the hall to greet him. He struggled to maintain his balance as they barked and hurled themselves at him, covering him with dog slobber.

They surrounded him, and when Gretchen came around behind him and pushed against the backs of his knees, he went down. "Hey, you guys!" he protested as they whined and licked every available inch of exposed skin. Paws the size of soup ladles scrabbled over him. Ears flapped in his face. And above the clamor he could hear the sweetest sound.

Dallas was laughing. Dallas, who had once claimed to hate chaos, seemed able to handle it just fine. He liked to think that his unrestrained loving the past few months had something to do with her relaxed attitude.

He pushed away Gretchen and her four puppies, each the size of a midsize dog at four months. There, leaning in the entrance to the hall, was his wife. He'd been away for two weeks and it seemed a lifetime. Every trip got harder. He'd turned down two assignments that would have taken him out of the country.

A puppy surged forward, blocking his view, and he shoved it back so he could look at her and watch the way her eyes danced as she smiled down at him. "Hi," he said.

"Welcome back." Her face glowed, and he knew that glow was in his honor.

"I see we still have four."

"Considering we started out with ten, that's not so bad."

He managed to get to his feet, although both his shoelaces were now untied and the front of his shirt was soaked with puppy drool. They'd inherited that from the Saint Bernard side of the family. "You guys are going out," he said, heading back toward the door.

"It's raining," Dallas reminded him gently. "They'll get muddy."

Gabe weighed the options. It was August, so they might get muddy, but they wouldn't get chilled. "I'll hose them down later," he said, opening the door. All five dogs bounded joyfully into the rain.

He closed the door and turned to find Dallas right beside him. "I'm covered with—"

She threw herself into his arms, cutting off his protest. "As if I care," she whispered against his mouth before claiming it in a greedy kiss.

He savored his return to paradise and wondered how he'd ever find the strength to leave when the next assignment came along. "Lord, I've missed you," he murmured when they came up for air.

"More than last time?"

"Much more." He eased away and glanced down at her gently rounded belly. "How are you feeling?"

"Wonderful."

"You're sure? Because if working at Rowdy Ranch is any problem, we could hire—"

"Gabe." She gave him a warning look.

He sighed. "Okay, but promise me you'll hire a replacement if you have any problems."

She smoothed the frown from between his eyebrows. "I think I promised that already. A few times. One of the reasons this works is that you can trust me to take care of myself when you're away."

He stroked his fingers through her hair. "And you want to know something stupid? I find myself wishing you weren't so self-sufficient, that you'd beg me to stay home more, so I'd have a good excuse not to go." He paused and stared at her. "I can't believe I just admitted that."

She gazed into his eyes, a soft smile on her face. "If we're making confessions, I'll admit that it tears my heart out each time you go, but I try not to show it. I don't want to tie you down."

He groaned and pulled her close. "Tie me down," he whispered, nuzzling the tender spot behind her ear. "Tell me you can't live without me."

"I can't. But your job—"

"Is becoming less important with every day I spend loving you. And when the baby comes . . . I'll be cutting back, Dallas. I may even find some kind of law enforcement work that keeps me in Tucson all the time." He was amazed that the decision made his heart light and joyous.

"I thought you needed excitement," she said, arching into him.

"I do." Desire blended with love as his body pounded in anticipation. "And it's right here in my arms."

COMING NEXT MONTH

#517 HEART TO HEART Elise Title
The Hart Girls Book 3

Kate Hart desperately needed a new program director to keep the family TV station going. Enter bad boy Brody Baker—on a motorcycle!—*hardly* the ideal candidate. But Brody was Kate's last hope...and the last man she should trust her heart with.

#518 THE TWELVE GIFTS OF CHRISTMAS
Rita Clay Estrada

All Carly wanted for Christmas was Pete Cade. He was ready and willing...except for one thing. Carly didn't just want a yuletide lover—she wanted a year-round father for her daughter too. And when it came to commitment, Pete was a real Scrooge.

#519 HAPPY BIRTHDAY, BABY Leandra Logan

Karen Bradford was shocked to learn that her baby, whom she believed had died, had instead been adopted. She needed to find Wendy. Only Karen fell hard for Wendy's father. After his bitter divorce, Ross had avoided any personal relationships. Karen yearned for a complete family...if only Ross would let Karen love Wendy and *him.*

#520 STRANGE BEDPERSONS Jennifer Crusie

Nick Jamieson wasn't right for Tess Newhart—his career always came first. But she still wanted him, because at times he could be caring and generous and wonderful. And Nick had the best body she'd ever seen.... Too bad great sex wasn't enough to build a relationship on—or was it?

Where do you find hot Texas nights, smooth Texas charm and dangerously sexy cowboys?

Crystal Creek reverberates with the exciting rhythm of Texas. Each story features the rugged individuals who live and love in the Lone Star state.

"...Crystal Creek wonderfully evokes the hot days and steamy nights of a small Texas community...impossible to put down until the last page is turned."
—*Romantic Times*

"With each book the characters in Crystal Creek become more endearingly familiar. This series is far from formula and a welcome addition to the category genre."
—*Affaire de Coeur*

"Altogether, it couldn't be better."
—*Rendezvous*

Don't miss the next book in this exciting series. Look for
THE HEART WON'T LIE by MARGOT DALTON

Available in January wherever Harlequin books are sold.

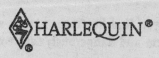

VOWS
Margaret Moore

Legend has it that couples who marry in the Eternity chapel are destined for happiness. Yet the couple who started it all almost never made it to the altar!

It all began in Eternity, Massachusetts, 1855....
Bronwyn Davies started life afresh in America and found refuge with William Powell. But beneath William's respectability was a secret that, once uncovered, could keep Bronwyn bound to him forever.

Don't miss **VOWS**, the exciting prequel to Harlequin's cross-line series, **WEDDINGS, INC.**, available in December from Harlequin Historicals. And look for the next **WEDDINGS, INC.** book, *Bronwyn's Story*, by Marisa Carroll (Harlequin Superromance #635), coming in March 1995.

WED7

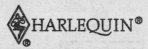

HARLEQUIN®

Don't miss these Harlequin favorites by some of our most distinguished authors!
And now you can receive a discount by ordering two or more titles!

HT#25483	BABYCAKES by Glenda Sanders	$2.99	☐
HT#25559	JUST ANOTHER PRETTY FACE by Candace Schuler	$2.99	☐
HP#11608	SUMMER STORMS by Emma Goldrick	$2.99	☐
HP#11632	THE SHINING OF LOVE by Emma Darcy	$2.99	☐
HR#03265	HERO ON THE LOOSE by Rebecca Winters	$2.89	☐
HR#03268	THE BAD PENNY by Susan Fox	$2.99	☐
HS#70532	TOUCH THE DAWN by Karen Young	$3.39	☐
HS#70576	ANGELS IN THE LIGHT by Margot Dalton	$3.50	☐
HI#22249	MUSIC OF THE MIST by Laura Pender	$2.99	☐
HI#22267	CUTTING EDGE by Caroline Burnes	$2.99	☐
HAR#16489	DADDY'S LITTLE DIVIDEND by Elda Minger	$3.50	☐
HAR#16525	CINDERMAN by Anne Stuart	$3.50	☐
HH#28801	PROVIDENCE by Miranda Jarrett	$3.99	☐
HH#28775	A WARRIOR'S QUEST by Margaret Moore	$3.99	☐
	(limited quantities available on certain titles)		

TOTAL AMOUNT	$
DEDUCT: 10% DISCOUNT FOR 2+ BOOKS	$
POSTAGE & HANDLING	$
($1.00 for one book, 50¢ for each additional)	
APPLICABLE TAXES*	$_____
<u>TOTAL PAYABLE</u>	$_____
(check or money order—please do not send cash)	

To order, complete this form and send it, along with a check or money order for the total above, payable to Harlequin Books, to: **In the U.S.:** 3010 Walden Avenue, P.O. Box 9047, Buffalo, NY 14269-9047; **In Canada:** P.O. Box 613, Fort Erie, Ontario, L2A 5X3.

Name: _____

Address: _____City: _____

State/Prov.: _____ Zip/Postal Code: _____

*New York residents remit applicable sales taxes.
 Canadian residents remit applicable GST and provincial taxes.

HBACK-OD

"HOORAY FOR HOLLYWOOD" SWEEPSTAKES

HERE'S HOW THE SWEEPSTAKES WORKS

OFFICIAL RULES — NO PURCHASE NECESSARY

To enter, complete an Official Entry Form or hand print on a 3" x 5" card the words "HOORAY FOR HOLLYWOOD", your name and address and mail your entry in the pre-addressed envelope (if provided) or to: "Hooray for Hollywood" Sweepstakes, P.O. Box 9076, Buffalo, NY 14269-9076 or "Hooray for Hollywood" Sweepstakes, P.O. Box 637, Fort Erie, Ontario L2A 5X3. Entries must be sent via First Class Mail and be received no later than 12/31/94. No liability is assumed for lost, late or misdirected mail.

Winners will be selected in random drawings to be conducted no later than January 31, 1995 from all eligible entries received.

Grand Prize: A 7-day/6-night trip for 2 to Los Angeles, CA including round trip air transportation from commercial airport nearest winner's residence, accommodations at the Regent Beverly Wilshire Hotel, free rental car, and $1,000 spending money. (Approximate prize value which will vary dependent upon winner's residence: $5,400.00 U.S.); 500 Second Prizes: A pair of "Hollywood Star" sunglasses (prize value: $9.95 U.S. each). Winner selection is under the supervision of D.L. Blair, Inc., an independent judging organization, whose decisions are final. Grand Prize travelers must sign and return a release of liability prior to traveling. Trip must be taken by 2/1/96 and is subject to airline schedules and accommodations availability.

Sweepstakes offer is open to residents of the U.S. (except Puerto Rico) and Canada who are 18 years of age or older, except employees and immediate family members of Harlequin Enterprises, Ltd., its affiliates, subsidiaries, and all agencies, entities or persons connected with the use, marketing or conduct of this sweepstakes. All federal, state, provincial, municipal and local laws apply. Offer void wherever prohibited by law. Taxes and/or duties are the sole responsibility of the winners. Any litigation within the province of Quebec respecting the conduct and awarding of prizes may be submitted to the Regie des loteries et courses du Quebec. All prizes will be awarded; winners will be notified by mail. No substitution of prizes are permitted. Odds of winning are dependent upon the number of eligible entries received.

Potential grand prize winner must sign and return an Affidavit of Eligibility within 30 days of notification. In the event of non-compliance within this time period, prize may be awarded to an alternate winner. Prize notification returned as undeliverable may result in the awarding of prize to an alternate winner. By acceptance of their prize, winners consent to use of their names, photographs, or likenesses for purpose of advertising, trade and promotion on behalf of Harlequin Enterprises, Ltd., without further compensation unless prohibited by law. A Canadian winner must correctly answer an arithmetical skill-testing question in order to be awarded the prize.

For a list of winners (available after 2/28/95), send a separate stamped, self-addressed envelope to: Hooray for Hollywood Sweepstakes 3252 Winners, P.O. Box 4200, Blair, NE 68009.

CBSRLS

OFFICIAL ENTRY COUPON

"Hooray for Hollywood"
SWEEPSTAKES!

Yes, I'd love to win the Grand Prize — a vacation in Hollywood —
or one of 500 pairs of "sunglasses of the stars"! Please enter me
in the sweepstakes!

This entry must be received by December 31, 1994.
Winners will be notified by January 31, 1995.

Name _____

Address _____ Apt. _____

City _____

State/Prov. _____ Zip/Postal Code _____

Daytime phone number _____
(area code)

Account # _____

Return entries with invoice in envelope provided. Each book
in this shipment has two entry coupons — and the more
coupons you enter, the better your chances of winning!

DIRCBS

OFFICIAL ENTRY COUPON

"Hooray for Hollywood"
SWEEPSTAKES!

Yes, I'd love to win the Grand Prize — a vacation in Hollywood —
or one of 500 pairs of "sunglasses of the stars"! Please enter me
in the sweepstakes!

This entry must be received by December 31, 1994.
Winners will be notified by January 31, 1995.

Name _____

Address _____ Apt. _____

City _____

State/Prov. _____ Zip/Postal Code _____

Daytime phone number _____
(area code)

Account # _____

Return entries with invoice in envelope provided. Each book
in this shipment has two entry coupons — and the more
coupons you enter, the better your chances of winning!

DIRCBS